THE STATION MASTER

Indranil Mukherjee

First published in 2018

Becomeshakespeare.com

Wordit Content Design & Editing Services Pvt Ltd
Unit - 26, Building A -1, Nr Wadala RTO,
Wadala (East), Mumbai 400037, India
T: +91 8080226699
Wordit Art Fund helps deserving authors publish their work by providing monetary support. To apply for funding, please visit us at www.BecomeShakespeare.com

ISBN - 978-93-88081-94-8

Disclaimer

Names of certain characters in the book and their identifying details have been changed to protect their privacy.

The author has made every effort to ensure the accuracy of the information within this book as relevant to the period when the stories are set. The author does not assume and hereby disclaims any liability to any party for any loss, damage, or disruption caused by errors or omissions, whether such errors or omissions result from accident, negligence, or any other cause.

To my wife,

Sanghamitra

For her constant encouragement…
oh, okay, for constantly being after me!
Without whom this book, therefore,
wouldn't have existed!

And,
To the Indian Railways

Preface

I heard a few of these stories at the dining table, over a meal that I consequently quite forgot to eat, despite being served a superb spread and being encouraged by word and gesture to tuck in by my cousin. The raconteur, a retired Indian Railways man, had finally given in to my wheedling, and was sharing a couple of incidents from his experience. So, as I said, I forgot to eat, so engrossed I had become in his narration. The one constant that buzzed in my mind was, "these need to be told!" Getting him—my source, Manas Banerjee—ready took some pursuing but then he reeled off a round ten. This book is the result of that.

There are no heroics here though you may discern heroisms, of a muted kind, tempered with common sense. The main protagonist of these ten stories is, instead, a man just like you and me, an ordinary Indian. In a career spanning over three and a half decades, in the heart of Bihar, he has had, however, to deal with the most extraordinary circumstances. He juggled danger, death, tragedy, resource crunch, time crisis, but dealt with them with common sense, dashes of humour, and always with humanity.

Manas Banerjee is Manab Banerjee in the stories, and with good reason. His Railways career in the stories spans exactly as it did in his life, from the time of his joining Indian Railways in 1976 till his retirement 35 years later. Among his many awards, Manas was twice, in 1992 and again in 1996, felicitated with the East Central Railway Zone General Manager's award for the Best Performer as station manager. In 2007 he was recognized as the Best Performer station manager and commended with the Minster of Railway's award.

Like in the book, he is married to a beautiful lady—my cousin—and they have three children, now each a young man or lady in his or her own right.

The stories are sequenced chronologically and Manab's personal life mimics Manas' fairly closely though not exactly; there are minor departures that affect the stories in no way. Reading the stories in sequence will give you, dear reader, a sense of Manab's life as it unfolded; individual stories may still be enjoyed stand-alone, though there may be occasional time jumps and a few back-references.

In keeping with Indian Railways norms, most references to time are shown in 24-hour format. The roles, designations, and technical descriptions are as accurate as I could make them without making them dreary. The other characters are accurate insofar as their connection with the stories are concerned but not in terms of their descriptions or their personalities and opinions: they are entirely mine and I own up to any divergences that may have crept in.

I have a whole lot of people to thank in this endeavour. Manas Banerjee, for spending hours narrating, repeating, and correcting, for explaining and re-explaining technical details, and then correcting them once more; for his infinite patience. For each of my reviewers, whether family, friends, or colleagues, for their words of advice, suggestions, encouragement, and criticism: Rima Mukherjee, Pavneet Kaur, Kaushik Majumdar, Lipika Ghosh, Nivedita Dhar, Srabasti Dutta, Sampriti Dutta, Arijit Dey Majumdar, Sanghamitra Mukherjee, Ayoush Mukherjee, and even my young nephew Rajdeep Mukherjee, all of 10 years but a great reader and an accomplished story-teller to boot. While writing maybe a lonely endeavour, getting it out before you is certainly not; it is a collective effort. To everyone, my sincerest thanks.

And to you, my dear reader, for picking this up when you could have picked any other.

Happy reading!

Indranil Mukherjee

May 2018

About the author

Indranil Mukherjee is an aspiring author of fiction but a long-time amateur writer, who has taken a break from his software career to give expression to his main passion: Writing. And if provided with timely sustenance to keep body and soul together, he loves to read. Besides these, he digs driving, travelling to all corners of the world, sampling all variety of food, meeting people, learning new stuff, listening to music, and about a couple of hundred other things. Curious about life, and armed with 25 years' worth of experience observing people from all over the world while working with them, he fancies he has stories to tell. Rather nifty ones.

Besides completing this collection of short stories based on an Indian Railways officer's real-life experiences--he already has a novelette eBook selling on Amazon titled "Re-Kill: when an assassin's professional pride is hurt..."--he has several works underway that comprise sci-fi, fantasy-humour-adventure, thriller, and has a maelstrom of other plots whirling in his head that occasionally meld nicely to create interesting dreams. And yes, a spot of scripting too.

Indranil is married to Sanghamitra, and they live in Delhi, while their son, Ayoush, has just started his career in the US.

He can be found at www.indranil-mukherjee.com where his blog lives, awaiting updates on life, the universe, and everything.

Contents

1
The Foundling

He shivered involuntarily as he stepped out of his home—two-roomed quarters with bare essentials that the Indian Railways had assigned him—into the gloomy night. Winter had set in well and truly, but he had the graveyard shift anyway. Remembering to lock the front door—though there was hardly anything that could be worth a thief's time—he greeted the wrapped-up porter waiting for him outside with a lantern. They spoke in *Magahi[1]*, the local language.

"All well, Hariya? Pretty cold, huh?"

"Yes *sahib[2]*, very cold. But will get colder, mark my word."

They started off for the railway station which was some distance away, exchanging chatter occasionally, shivering continually, the porter in front with his lamp swinging while he brought up the rear with a torchlight in his hand, the beam eerily bouncing off the swirling mist.

Early in the year 1976, Manab Banerjee had taken up his first posting as one of the three Assistant Station Masters of the railway station at Mokameh, a sleepy little town some 90 kilometres from the state capital city of Patna. The town of course had a 'reputation'; indeed, Bihar itself had a reputation. But he was born in Patna, grown up in the smaller towns of Bihar, mostly in Danapur, Patna's satellite town barely 13 kilometres away, spoke the local dialects like born

---

[1] Language spoken in about 18 districts of the undivided state of Bihar
[2] Akin to 'sir'

to them—which he was, in a manner of speaking—and lived the life of a Railway family member since his father was a doctor employed with the Indian Railways. So, neither the 'reputation' of the town nor the life of a Railway employee was new for him. His mother had demurred initially, but her heart had not been fully in it; she let him go with her blessings. His father had of course no qualms and had encouraged him with word and gesture.

He had been an average student but a fairly good sportsman, had often brought certain teachers to grief, and had never really promised to do anything spectacular. He had himself never really thought about building a career. He hadn't actively thought of anything; the Railway thing had come almost automatically and there was naturally no question of resisting or for thinking of anything else. He had gone through the formal hiring process of course, taken the test, faced the interview, and undergone the training. But not for a minute had it been an option to be picked from a bouquet of choices. It was the *only* option. Taking up the Railway job was the start of his career.

He had arrived in Mokameh with toothbrush and tin trunk in tow in February that year. Rameshwar Mishra, the Station Manager of Mokameh, took him under his ample wing and set about tuning him up for his responsibilities. Mishra was a friendly soul, generous with his advice and his lunchbox though the latter often ran short due to this generosity, what with the three ASMs under him. While the Station Manager had overall responsibility of the station, the ASMs had various supervisory responsibilities per their assigned shift hours, followed by the commercial staff who dealt with issuing tickets to passengers, booking freight; then there were a few porters who did a variety of work—including accompanying Manab from his home to the station in the dead of night with the lamp lighting the way—and the shuntmen who manoeuvred engines and trains in the network of tracks in and around the station.

The station itself was situated between the town proper and the railway colony with its standard, uniform quarters. Platform number 1, as is the usual layout plan with railway stations across the country, faced the town. There were four platforms in the station and beyond the fourth lay the railway colony. It was in this same colony that Manab had his quarters. Naturally, he walked to work every day, well, night, now that his duty hours had changed. The night shifts were special. The ASM was the king of all he surveyed. This of course meant he had to do all kinds of jobs since there was no commercial staff in the night, there were fewer porters and shuntmen. But the night shifts were enjoyable in their own way. There were far fewer passengers, disruptions, or crises to handle. Lot of paperwork could be accomplished mostly without interruptions.

He had had the day shift for three months upon joining after which Mishra decided he was trained and experienced enough to be on his own for the night shift. That he was the junior most of the ASMs might also have crossed his mind. Not only had Manab's shift timings changed but recently even his responsibilities had: he had been taken off platform duties and been made in-charge of the East Cabin.

Those days, when signals were mostly manual and track changings entirely so, cabins were important outposts of control. Each station had just such a cabin situated on either side, from where both entry and exit of trains were controlled. They were high single storeyed buildings with large windows facing the tracks. The main feature was the largish room filled with levers that needed to be manipulated to move the tracks. Then the in-charge would take a green flag or a green lamp and lean out of the window to signal safe passage for the passing train.

In the beginning, he would start his night shift anxiously, carefully taking over from the previous cabin in-charge, making notes, annotations on those notes, reconfirming, but as he got used to it, his anxiety lessened. He even started to enjoy his lonely vigils. There weren't as many trains in any case.

The day time shift had its own peculiarities that needed prudent handling. And exceptions that needed to be addressed. One of the recurring things was apprehending passengers travelling without ticket—termed 'travelling WT'—who would bizarrely profess loss of face if they're expected to *buy* tickets! These were not penniless villagers, rather, they were often very rich landowners, farmers who had money by the sacksful. Manab had found that an amusing peculiarity but it had taken him a while to wrap his mind around the issue. Naturally, these passengers were locals alighting off trains and were expected to handover the tickets to the ticket collectors at the exit points as proof of having travelled with valid tickets. The collectors were expected to manage this but there were frequent 'escalations' and the ASM on duty was called in to arbitrate.

Manab had thought of it as a straightforward matter: ticketless passenger apprehended, penalty to be imposed. To his surprise, at least initially, the WT traveller would unhesitatingly, almost cheerfully, pay the money. Translated into numbers, it meant for a ticket worth two rupees the passenger was willing to pay two hundred and fifty rupees! The typical interaction went something like this:

"You've arrived by this train, right, sir?"

"Or what? This is the only train on the platform so where else would I've sprung from?" This would be usually accompanied by an indignant look.

"Exactly, sir. May I see your ticket then please?"

More astonishment would register on the passenger's face as if it was a completely idiotic question.

"Ticket? Ticket? What would I have a ticket for?"

"Er… to travel?"

"Please! Buy ticket? And lose all respect?"

At this point, Manab would blanch—against all logic—and stutter, "Lose respect? Why would you lose respect, sir?"

An indignant hand on his chest, the passenger would bristle. "How can I not lose respect! Don't you know who I am?"

This of course is the very Indian tradition that we still are privileged to enjoy. The expectation that others would know the asker's pedigree has been well ingrained.

Manab often urged to ask with a straight face, "Why, sir? Would you need some help to find out?" But curbed the thought.

Instead, he would ask, "I don't understand, sorry, sir! Please help me understand?"

Puffing up further, the irate one would say, "Me? Stand in some filthy queue to buy tickets? And have the entire town know I—*I* stood in a line? Like any common man? And have my nose cut in public humiliation? Bah!"

Reason faltered. Comprehension dithered. In the early days, of course. Later he took these in his stride. But then, in those early days, he floundered for a response.

"B-but… without ticket travel is an offence, sir, against the government rules! And now you have to pay a penalty!"

Glee would register on the WT passenger's face, contrary to all sense. Lifting his long white shirt up to his waist, he would unroll an ample bundle tucked in his pyjama-hose to reveal an unwieldy and large wad of currency notes of all denominations. Peeling off a few notes, he'd proudly exclaim, "This is respect! Now people will know I travelled in real style!"

A dazed Manab would collect the penalty money, issue the receipt, and let the triumphant passenger go, beaming, good humour restored.

As he passed the slow nights, he would sometimes recollect snatches of such droll experiences and chuckle quietly to himself. Life could be odd.

Beyond both the cabins stood a system of signals which were controlled from there. The cabins themselves stood almost a kilometre from the station, one to the east and the other to the west. A kilometre from the cabin stood the Home signal and another kilometre beyond, the Outer signal. And similarly, the Starter signal was placed about a kilometre beyond the other cabin, and the Advanced Starter another kilometre out from there. The Outer and Home signals controlled the entry of incoming trains at the assigned platform based on the berthing plan made by the SM, while the Starter and Advanced Starter signals controlled the exit. The Outer signal was interlinked with the previous station's exit point Advanced Starter. This system ensured a generally fail-safe mechanism for safe rail transport.

The area between the Home signal and the east cabin was piled high with steam engine coal ash, at points these were several feet high, creating veritable little hills. In the day time, they appeared just what they were: piles of ash. But at night, in the moonlight, one might be walking in a gully, the sides ashy-blue and occasionally, eerie. For reasons unknown, they had never been cleared and now they were a permanent feature of the landscape. Farther along the rail tracks, there were the sparse woods, some scrubland and then the flood-prone plains, rich with alluvial deposits from the annual floods. They gathered rich harvests of crops and cash from these fertile lands, enabling those proud farmers to fund their extravagant notions of respect vis-à-vis WT travel.

The station itself was the standard issue small-town setup. The main platform, number 1, was the hub around which all activities revolved. There was the usual A.H. Wheeler's, the ubiquitous chain of station bookstores, a couple of food stalls that sold standard railway fare, the waiting rooms, offices of the railway staff, the GRP,[3] the RPF,[4] SM's office. *Coolies*[5] hung around from early morning till about late evening and of course, throngs of people, passengers and non-passengers, gawkers, and vendors. That's the definitive feature of any Indian railway station… the masses of people. Whole families turn up to see off a single traveller or to receive them, platform tickets never quite an effective deterrent.

---

[3] Government Railway Police
[4] Railway Protection Force
[5] Porters who carry baggage for passengers for a fee

The other platforms were far less in every aspect barring perhaps the length! Less crowded, fewer food stalls, maybe one book stall on wheels, a few lonely, thin, shrivelled trees, and often no corrugated tin roof. Even fewer coolies and vendors; they went over when passenger trains halted there.

Manab could see the glimmerings of light from the station; the mist here was tendrils of floating gossamer. A chilly breeze, blowing very gently, had shredded the mist. In the light from the porter's lantern, the ash heaps appeared mysterious undulations but the harsher light from his torchlight dispelled the mystery, indeed made them look flat, grey, and ugly. They were walking their usual trail to the east cabin. A narrow path, worn to prominence with regular use, led from the lane at the edge of the railway colony up over a grassy verge to the rocky bed of the rail tracks.

"Hariya, did Baranwal hand over the files to Pankaj?" Manab focussed on his upcoming tasks. Dhiraj Baranwal was the cabin in-charge who handled the 0800 hours-1600 hours shift[6]. When he had left in the morning that day, he had left the files for some regular updates to be made by Baranwal, who, in turn, would have handed them over to Pankaj Kumar, who handled the 1600 hours- midnight shift. Manab would take over those from Pankaj when he took over at the start of that night's shift from midnight.

"Yes, *sahib*, he had completed what you'd asked him to," Hariya answered.

"Hmm," grunted Manab, walking steadily, still behind Hariya and his welcome lamplight. The cabin was perhaps another quarter of a kilometre ahead.

Just then a plaintive wail rang through the night behind them. Manab sighed.

"That cat needs to move her litter out of the cold, Hariya."

[6] Cabin duty hours were set 2 hours off from station duty hours for the sake of 2-hour overlap for continuity purposes

Hariya laughed softly. "Who'll tell her, *sahib*? She's a very independent minded cat!"

Manab smiled to himself. This was a common cat that had recently delivered a litter of rather fetching kittens that mewled loudly day and night from various points around the east cabin. Apparently, the mother foraged far and wide to keep her little family fed and during her prolonged absences the kittens raised quite a ruckus.

Another wail sounded. It was some distance behind them, beyond the point where the path crossed over the tracks and turned towards the cabin. Something in the nature of the wail gave Manab pause.

"Hariya! The cry sounds different, don't you think?" He turned around and waved the beam of his torchlight behind. There was nothing of note; the grey mounds of ash stared back. No movement, nothing.

Hariya had also stopped. He too raised the lantern and peered into the distance behind them.

"*Sahib*, the cry was that of a kitten in distress, what else?"

He turned around and said over his shoulder, "Come *sahib*, it's getting to your shift start time, Pankaj-*sahib* will be waiting…" and he walked on.

Manab too did not linger any longer. He tried to pin down what had sounded different in the wail, but it eluded him. Anyway, he *knew* there were cats around. Perhaps the ash heaps had caused some distortion in the cries, making them sound… what, *human*, to a degree?

"Bah!" he exclaimed softly to himself and walked on.

Pankaj Kumar was wrapping up his shift when they reached. The greeting was perfunctory, and quickly explaining the needs of the shift, he left for home and sleep. The nightly ritual for Manab was something he looked forward to: Hariya prepared a flask of milky tea, poured him a tall glass of it for starters and a plate of glucose biscuits. Manab would savour those while glancing through the berthing plan for the night, the train schedules and other routine stuff. Usually a quick telephone call to the ASM at the station also featured in the list of settling-in activities.

The first train set to pass at 0035 hours on his watch was the 49 Up. There was another passenger train scheduled to arrive at Mokameh at 0225 hours. There were several freight trains thereafter until about 0510 hours when another express would pass through.

He had done his tea and had prepared for the 49 Up. It was running a few minutes late and thus it proved to be when it was cleared around 0050 hours. There was an hour until the next one, the first of the freighters, that required his attention. Hariya had gone from the cabin for a while, and it was in that state, alone and free, that he was reminded of the wail he'd heard earlier that night.

That was the point, he thought. The difference that was eluding him had struck him then too, but he had dismissed that as absurd. The wail had sounded human… he thought about it a bit and it seemed, thinking rationally, while it might have sounded human there was no chance of it being anything else but of feline origin! The night, mist, those damn ash heaps… they all combined to distort the sound, he was sure. He scoffed mentally.

Human! Crazy! Who in his right mind would take a child out for a stroll in that kind of cold… and that time of the night? Absurd!

He lit a cigarette, an unfiltered *Charminar*[7]. Blowing a satisfying ring of smoke out, he chuckled. Imagination, coupled with the right atmosphere, could be a potent story-maker!

Hariya clattered up the staircase just then and opened the door, causing a blast of cold to blow in behind him. Manab grinned at him.

"Hariya, you know what I was thinking of? That wail we heard while coming to the cabin."

He looked a bit troubled but Manab didn't quite notice.

"Yes, *sahib*…"

───────────────

[7] A brand of usually unfiltered cigarettes, very popular in the yesteryears

"Yes! And I was thinking it almost human! Can you imagine that?" He laughed, a tinge of embarrassment evident.

Hariya appeared more flustered but Manab was too absorbed in the absurdity of this imagination to notice. Hariya started, "That's what I…" but was interrupted by Manab.

"It's obviously not, Hariya! Just cannot be! Think about it, who'd, in his right mind, take a child out at this time of the night and in such cold?"

He waved his arm deprecatingly. "I'm sure the landscape there along with the mist distorted the sound… the cat would laugh derisively if it learnt of my imagination!"

"But *sahib*…" Hariya started to say but paused.

That got Manab's attention. "Eh?" He focussed on the porter. "You appear agitated Hariya? What's the matter?"

"It's Nandu sir, you know, the night duty porter at the station?"

Nandu was a porter who had been on night duty for ages. That he had 5 children despite that caused much comment and ribald humour around. Of course Manab knew him.

"Of course. What about him?"

Animation sent a series of expressions flitting across Hariya's face. He said, "I went to the station just now sir, you know, and I met Nandu there. He'd just arrived for his shift!"

He made it sound quite momentous. He carried on without needing further encouragement. "Nandu takes the same route as us *sahib*… he passed by the same spot as us! And…" he paused presumably for some dramatic effect.

Manab could guess of course but he didn't spoil it for Hariya. "And?" He prodded gently.

Eyes popping, Hariya breathed, "He heard that caterwauling too, *sahib*!"

Manab smiled. Snuffing out the smoked-to-the-butt cigarette, he responded mildly, "If he takes the same route and passed by that spot soon after us then it is likely he'd have heard that… so what's the big deal?"

The big deal moment had come for Hariya. Emphasising his point with his forefinger, he said, in a grating whisper, "That's the point, *sahib*! He too said its human!"

Now, Nandu was an incorrigible gossip and tended to colour his stories rather shamelessly. If a man was pickpocketed of, say, five rupees, he would say the man was robbed of fifty, or maybe even mugged by a gang of thugs, beaten up and robbed penniless. In this case it was natural for him to claim it was a child; a kitten mewling was simply no story.

Laughing out aloud, Manab exclaimed, "Of all the people, Hariya, Nandu would claim that!" He got up and stretched. "In fact, now that Nandu has claimed it was human we can all relax and be certain it's really the cat!"

While he was reconfirming the next train's passing time, Hariya said, "Exactly, *sahib*, I know his nature and that's the reason I challenged him… but he swore on his dead mother!"

Still amused, Manab said over his shoulder, "I wouldn't expect any less from him, Hariya! He's just the sort to do that… that gas-bag!" He brusquely shuffled some papers and continued briskly, "Now Hariya, we've work to do. There's almost an hour till the freighter comes along so let's get them done, okay?"

"Yes, sir." Hariya was a fairly conscientious worker and he leaned in without murmur.

They were absorbed in their tasks, but the initial thought still rankled in Manab's mind. After a few minutes of battling that, he gave up with a curse and lit a cigarette.

"Hariya, let's go and check it out, shall we?"

He knew instinctively what Manab meant but he still asked to confirm. "What, *sahib*?"

"That wailing, what else?"

A shadow of fear crossed Hariya's face. Manab was curious. "Why are you afraid?"

There was a distinct quaver in his voice now. Hariya said, "*Sahib*, it's not safe! What if it's not a cat but neither human? What if it's a *chudail*[8]?"

"Bah!" Exasperation was thick in Manab's tone. The certainty of youth bypassed the room for doubt quite emphatically. He said severely: "Don't give old wives tales to me, Hariya! *Chudail*, for God's sake! There're no such things. Now come with me with your lamp and let's settle this once and for all."

Hariya's expression was stricken. "*Sahib*! You haven't seen them, but I have! Feet are backward, too! No sir, it's too dangerous, please don't risk it yourself!"

Manab paid no attention to Hariya's frantic pleadings. He put his jacket back on, picked up his torchlight and announced quietly, "I'm going, Hariya. Are you coming or not?"

Hariya was visibly torn between his fears and his devotion to duty though the former was ahead by some margin at the moment. "*Sahib*, please believe me! These *chudail* can spoil your life, completely destroy your happiness!"

Manab glared coldly. "I'm going, come if you wish." And he moved out of the door into the cold.

As he reached the bottom of the stairs, Hariya clambered out of the cabin and climbed down.

"So you're coming after all, good."

"*Sahib*, if you've to go then please let's take another couple of people with us from the station, please listen to me!" He pleaded.

---

[8] Female ghost, reputedly much given to cackling laughter; also, refers to a witch

Their breath fogged, wisps escaping as they spoke. Seeing the look of pleading and his plaintive cry, Manab relented a bit.

"Okay, here's what we'll do then. Let's take Nandu along as well, okay?" With that he turned towards the station that lay ahead. "And oh, arm yourselves with stout sticks… just in case!" He laughed aloud and strode off.

Despite deep misgivings Hariya scrambled after him. Stout sticks… against *chudail*!

They got hold of Nandu at the end of platform 1 where he was going about some task but getting him to agree was almost impossible. Manab didn't care if either of them declined; he had no time for superstitions. Now that he had set out to settle the matter he would brook no opposition or hindrance. At the end it was Hariya who convinced Nandu to go along. As Manab walked off, Hariya whispered fiercely to Nandu telling him his job could be in danger if he failed to back up his claims of having heard a human being wailing earlier that night. They grabbed a couple of stout bamboos and ran after the receding figure of the east cabin in-charge, trepidation intact.

Manab set a scorching pace. The beam from his torchlight was enough to light his path and when the two porters caught up with him, their lamps added to it. They passed the cabin, Manab automatically glancing up with unseeing eyes. They pressed on. The ash heaps loomed up and just then, a cry sounded, feebler than before but clear nevertheless.

It definitely sounded some distance away. They broke into a gentle lope, careful not to run between the tracks. Manab swept his torchlight at the nooks and crannies caused by the tumble of the heaps. There was nothing to spot. Yet.

They crossed many heaps with no luck and no wails. A cold fear gripped Manab. What if it was indeed a human… and in this cold? He took a grip on himself and proceeded further, Hariya and Nandu close behind. They were petrified, eyes frantic and agape, holding their sticks in a grip that caused their knuckles to stand out white.

A light breeze had again sprung up and they shivered. Manab had stopped at a spot where the heaps had run such that there were several gulches between the shallow peaks. He peeked and poked to no avail when suddenly, possibly borne on the breeze, came a faint whimper. They froze, Manab desperately trying to locate the source.

"S-*Sahib*!" Nandu stammered fearfully. "*Sahib*, I think it came from the other side of the line!"

The heaps were on either side of the tracks of course. Manab focussed: could Nandu be right? Well, he jolly well could be. The only way to confirm was to go check. He turned and hurried across the tracks.

The undulating sea of mounds confronted them on this side too and with equal lack of success. There were no wails; Manab was willing them to restart so that they might locate the spot. A keen desperation had taken hold of him. He flicked his torchlight wildly.

Chance took pity on him. A plaintive cry sounded again and to Manab's fevered imagination it sounded frantic, in distress.

"Did you hear that?" he asked agitatedly, shining the beam on the faces of the porters who blinked and nodded.

"Y-yes, *sahib*!" Hariya's tone was fearful.

The wail had sounded uncannily human. The unspoken word hovered over them all: *chudail!*

But Manab paid no heed. He pointed to the other side. "It's coming from there! Come!" And he ran across.

They went over square foot by painful square foot. The path from the colony side that Manab took every day lay behind them by several yards. Suddenly Manab shushed his companions and bent forward, ears pricked: he thought he had heard a faint whimper.

And in answer to his urgent prayers they all heard another whimper, louder than before and best of all, they knew exactly where it was coming from. They all looked at the mound in front of them in wild surmise.

Another faint whimper sounded, timed to perfection it seemed to Manab for them to track it down while the porters thought the *chudail* had sprung the trap perfectly timed.

"There!" Manab pointed his torchlight at a spot where the heap formed a trough. It rose a few feet away to form the next heap, but his attention was sharply focussed at the trough. From this distance nothing was visible. He stepped forward, heart thudding. What would he find?

A shallow hole had been dug, the edges raised slightly. As Manab's torchlight lit the spot up he drew his breath sharply. Swaddled in thick cloths lay a new born baby, perhaps no more than a day or two old. *Human* baby. Its eyes were screwed shut, mouth twisted in a silent cry. It had managed to pull one hand out of its tight wrapping and was using that to rub its eyes.

"Good God!" breathed Manab.

Nandu and Hariya had also crept up beside him but their superstitious fear was not yet gone.

Hariya's voice had a quaver. "*Sahib*, this is an illusion! Please don't touch it!"

He obviously still wasn't prepared to abandon the *chudail* line of thought. He gathered his courage to speak once again to his boss who looked on entranced at the baby.

"*Sahib, chudail* work like this, they cast spells..."

He was rudely interrupted when Manab exclaimed sharply, "Shut up, Hariya!" and without waiting for any further objections, he carefully picked the baby up, wrappings and all. The porters' protests died on their lips.

"Pick the torchlight up!" he brusquely ordered them and turning around, started walking back towards the cabin and station.

Manab felt a strange, urgent need to hurry. He had no idea how one tended to as young a baby and this one had suffered possibly several hours of exposure to the cold. Instinct told him warm milk was needed and a warm bed too. How would either be done he again had no clue but it sure had to be done.

He walked directly into the SM's office. There had been hardly anyone on the platform then. The baby had fallen asleep in his arms, possibly comforted by his body warmth and the rhythmic rocking as he had run, carefully but hurriedly. Hariya and Nandu were quiet, dumbstruck by the miracle of finding a human baby amongst the ash heaps and wonder of wonders, one that had not shape-shifted to a cackling *chudail*.

Kapil Tiwari, the night shift ASM at the station, was dozing at his desk. It was an uneventful night… or, unbeknownst to him yet, had been one till then. He opened a bulbous eye sensing the sudden appearance of people in his office.

"Tiwari-ji!" The urgency in Manab's voice conveyed itself to the dozing ASM. His eyes cleared.

"Eh?" He hadn't found speech yet.

"Tiwari-ji! Look what I've found!"

Tiwari transitioned to full awakening in a couple of seconds. Since Manab had not laid the child on the desk, still cradling it in his arms, Tiwari couldn't see anything. He jumped up and alarm spread across his face rapidly.

"Where did you find it?" His voice was a high falsetto in shock and anxiety.

A natural sense of protectiveness caused Manab to swing away from the agitated Tiwari.

"Lower your voice, dammit! You'll awaken him!"

Tiwari, suitably chastened, merely gestured with his hands. Where did you find it?

Manab rapidly narrated the entire episode with occasional corroborations from the porters. He concluded it by insisting on some hot milk and a blanket.

"Listen, Manab, while it is good you have retrieved the baby from the ash heaps, this is a police case! We have to inform the GRP!"

"We'll take care of all formalities but first things first! This baby needs food and warmth! Organize them!" Without waiting for Tiwari's response, he whirled around at Hariya and Nandu.

"Fetch some hot milk, now! I don't care where you find it but get it!"

As the bemused porters started to leave, Manab added, "Wait! Go to the tea stall and wake Ghanshyam up! He'll be sure to have some milk left over for his early morning tea making... get hold of that from him!"

Only Tiwari and Manab were left in the office once the porters left. Manab continued to cradle the baby, the protective urge yet to dissipate. Tiwari nerved himself to bring up the topic of the formalities that Manab had been so dismissive about a few minutes back.

"*Dada*[9]," he addressed Manab gently.

Manab was of course the universal '*Dada*', the inescapable honorific for a Bengali gentleman of any age. True to all clichés, irrespective of age, everyone called him that, barring of course the junior staff like the porters and shuntmen.

Manab raised his eyebrows in response.

"I mean, *dada*, we need to get the formalities done… for the baby, you know. We've to get the GRP involved and…"

---

[9] Literally, elder brother, in the Bengali language

He was interrupted. "Yes, we will, of course." He paused, a sudden thought striking. "What on earth has to be done? I mean, with the GRP, for the baby?"

Tiwari was quiet for a moment, evidently struggling to assess possibilities then shook his head. "No, don't know at all, can't guess either!"

Manab nodded but attempted thinking aloud. "I guess they'll expect an FIR[10]…" He sighed. "The child will then probably be taken to some orphanage…" for an unknown future…" his voice petered out as if he could see the bleak future.

They stood quiet, the moment deep in some indeterminate pathos. Then Manab shook himself, something unquantifiable wanting to grab his attention.

"What time is it, Tiwari-ji?"

By the time Tiwari responded, Manab knew what was burgeoning for expression within.

"Just… just past 0200 hours, *dada*!"

"The 210 Up!" Manab would have clapped his head if his hands had been free. "It's due at 0225 hours!"

He scrambled. "Quick! Hold the baby…" Tiwari was a married man with a baby himself, so he was not a novice at holding babies; he did so without question.

"And," continued Manab, "when Hariya is back with the milk, feed him!" And with a phrase that was yet to gain universal popularity, "I'll be back!" he left hurriedly, sprinting away into the darkness.

Manab came back to the SM's office about forty minutes later, after having ushered in the 201 Up to platform 1. He had some time on hand before he needed to be back in the cabin. By rights he ought

---

[10] First Information Report; lodged with the police to register a case

not to have been out of there but tonight was a rather different one, a special night.

Inside, there were a few more people now than before. Tiwari had cleared out the desk to make place for the baby who was now sleeping peacefully, wrapped in a relatively cleaner blanket. Besides Tiwari, there was the GRP sub inspector Kishan Yadav, a man in his thirties with a quizzical expression now compounded by signs of worry; there also stood Ghanshyam, the tea stall man, dishevelled and bemused and beside him stood Kamla, his wife, looking curious but calm. Apparently, someone had had the wit to fetch her to clean up the baby, feed it and wrap it back in a cleaner blanket. Hariya was of course back in the east cabin; Manab had rejected his hesitant request to be back here saying someone had to be present in the cabin. Nandu had no doubt been sent back to his normal duties.

Manab was taking in the tableau quietly when Yadav spoke up.

"*Dada*!" You couldn't expect anything else. "You've done a miracle! You've saved a new life… you were God's hand! But…" his voice trailed off, only now matching the expression on his face.

For now, Manab ignored him and turned towards Kamla. He spoke gently.

"Kamla-ji, thank you for caring for the baby."

Kamla squirmed in embarrassment but was evidently happy for the recognition given her.

It struck him just then that he still did not know if it was a boy or a girl. He asked that of Tiwari who said it was a boy. Only then he turned towards the fretting Yadav.

"Yadav-ji, what do we need to do to take care of this baby?"

The sub inspector was clearly unhappy with the situation. "Care? What do you mean? You want to adopt the baby?"

Manab was taken aback. He had certainly not meant that. He said, rather aggressively, "Me? How can I adopt a baby? How will I care for it? I'm not married either!" Taking a deep breath, he forced himself to speak calmly.

"Listen, Yadav-ji. All we want to know now is how do we ensure this baby is safely handed over to some orphanage?"

Yadav lit a cigarette. He sat down, sighed, and then asked, "First, I need to know how you found the child."

This was astonishing! Manab bristled. "Surely you've already heard how I found this baby?"

When Manab glared at Tiwari, the latter nodded guiltily. "Yes *dada*, I explained that to him… whatever you told me!"

Manab whirled back at Yadav. "So?"

Yadav stared. "No, no… I want to hear from you."

So Manab started with the story resignedly. It was plain that his tale tallied in all essential aspects with the version Yadav had heard from Tiwari. But they were back to wrangling with the immediate future of the baby at the end of the narration. For all practical purposes, the basic objection that Yadav had was the administrative paperwork involved. And which frustrated Manab no end. How much work could that really involve!

Yadav kept sighing. "*Dada*, you've landed me in so much unnecessary work…" he grumbled.

Meanwhile, Tiwari quietly spoke to Ghanshyam and Kamla, letting them go with the warning that Kamla might be needed again. Manab nodded to them as they left.

"Yadav-ji, I found an abandoned child, possibly left there by some unfortunate unwed mother from the Umavati Hospital… there are witnesses to my finding the baby in the ash heaps… and there he is… all you have to do is to mark the baby as abandoned then send him over to the orphanage! That's all!"

"On the contrary, *dada*! I'd have to make a case, run an investigation, try to find the parents… too much work!"

"What's happened?"

A new voice behind startled them. They turned around towards the entrance in unison and saw Dilip Biswas standing there with his mouth hanging open and eyes opened wide.

Dilip Biswas was a familiar figure to each of them. In his mid-thirties, he was a train guard on the 201 Up, and lived in Mokameh. On certain nights, his duty hours ended when his train reached Mokameh. He would then get off and go home, usually after spending a few minutes gassing with the ASM and a few other staff present then. This night too he must have ended his shift and had come over to the SM's office for the usual gossip.

"Ah, Biswas-*da*[11]!" Manab greeted him, recovering first from the interruption. "Duty over?"

Biswas had spotted the baby lying on the desk and his attention was completely focussed there. He merely nodded in reply and pointed at the sleeping baby. The question was obvious.

With a sigh, Manab narrated the whole story again, this time with a few interjections and corroborations from both Tiwari and Yadav. Biswas listened with rapt attention, eyes seldom straying from the baby. Once Manab completed his account, Biswas had only one question.

"What'll you do with the baby?"

All eyes turned naturally towards Yadav who appeared defensive.

"Yadav-ji will organize the necessary paperwork to ensure the baby is taken in by an orphanage at the earliest." Manab pre-empted Yadav's objections.

---

[11] Shortened form of 'dada'

Yadav started to quibble again. In exasperation, Manab asked of him, "Then what do you suggest, Yadav-ji? We abandon the child yet again? Is that what you want?"

He was feeling upset, frustrated by useless objections and the sheer unwillingness to do the right thing.

Yadav could obviously not say that outright. He also knew the only step for him would be to register the foundling and follow through with the case to its conclusion. And in his years with the police, he knew such abandoned babies could seldom be traced to parents unwilling to acknowledge the new born.

Tiwari suggested contacting the Umavati Hospital to inquire if they were missing a baby. Maybe they would have also informed the local police of such a missing baby already? What then?

Manab scoffed at the idea. His frustration, coupled with a strange feeling of responsibility for the helpless little life, caused him to be brusque, something not quite natural for him.

"Gentlemen! Why can't we try to do the right thing instead of focussing on following the 'right procedures'? Saving a life should be the most important aspect in this entire matter!"

There was shocked silence with perhaps a trace of embarrassment on the faces of Yadav and Tiwari.

Manab toned his voice down. "Okay, I admit confirming the disappearance of a baby from the hospital is perhaps important, let's do that. But, can we not first ensure it is put somewhere where it can be taken care of till such investigation is completed?"

The idea was obviously sensible. Manab felt they could be persuaded. He was about to speak again, hoping to nudge them over, when Biswas spoke up.

"I say!" His eyes were alight and his whole appearance spoke of shivers of excitement coursing through him.

"I say!" Biswas said in a hushed voice. "I've an idea... an idea that could avoid all problems and help the child as all of us want!"

They all looked at him expectantly. "What is it?" Manab voiced everyone's query.

Biwas took a deep breath, as if preparing himself for something momentous.

"Give the child to me! Let me adopt him!"

The other three were too dumbstruck to speak. Biswas felt compelled to elaborate.

"You know we're childless. My wife grieves for one... God has not taken mercy on us! Perhaps he is now answering our prayers!"

That was something everyone knew. Biswas and his wife Chandrima were indeed childless. They had heard many times their sorrow at not having a child despite medical check-ups and religious entreaties and that his wife was often low.

But this?

Manab didn't know how quite to respond. How could Biswas just *take* the child away!

"How can that be done!" Manab whispered. He looked at Tiwari and Yadav for their reaction. They too appeared dazed.

Something told Biswas that he was on a possible good wicket. He pressed on, earnest in his manner, driven by the vision of sudden fulfilment of their deeply desired dream.

"Trust me! Please believe me! We... my wife and I... we'll take all care of the baby! We'll bring him up as our own son! Trust me!"

He looked wildly with hope at each one of them, a half smile, hopeful in every seam, curved his mouth.

Before anyone else, Yadav spoke. "It is a good idea!"

Manab looked at him in surprise. That was least expected. Even Tiwari looked mystified.

Yadav continued. "Why not, Biswas-dada! I know you both, you're good people!"

A sneaky thought occurred to Manab: was Yadav agreeing because that would reduce his burden?

He said, "Biswas-da, you've come up with a surprising idea…" He paused.

Biswas jumped in. "I know what you might be thinking. What's the guarantee that we'd look after the child properly… but consider this: what's the guarantee that he would grow up better in some orphanage? Or would be adopted by some people who none know?"

As they all paused, he looked at each of them, quickly moving his head. "At least you know me… you know my wife! Isn't that a better chance?"

Manab came to a decision suddenly. He focussed on Yadav.

"Yadav-ji, but we'd need to check for a missing baby, right? Just in case?"

Yadav slammed his fist into his palm. "Of course! I'll do that myself! Not officially but through my contacts, in a personal capacity! *Pucca*[12]*!*"

Biswas chimed in as if on cue. "Please do that! And I assure you if the parents are found… and they want the child back, we'd return him right away…"

"Hmm…" Manab thought for a long moment. It was as if, as the finder, he had responsibility to take the final call.

"*Dada…*" Tiwari began when Biswas interrupted vigorously.

"Manab, my friend, I'll give my assurances in writing!"

---

[12] For certain

And that's how it turned. Biswas wrote a few lines on a plain sheet of paper, an oath to nourish, cherish, and bring the child up as his own and in case his parents were found he'd hand over the baby to them. Manab insisted Tiwari and Yadav also sign that along with himself as witnesses, which they did with some reluctance. Manab promised to hold the paper with himself privately. After this, which under the circumstances, seemed to give the entire proceedings a sense of solemnity, there was little left to be done.

Biswas carefully lifted the baby up in his arms as if it was a bundle of treasures, awkwardly shook hands with each one of them and left with unstinted happiness oozing from his whole being. Manab was surprised to feel his eyes go prickly with sudden tears. After Biswas had gone, and they were all feeling a little dazed, Manab decided he needed to be back in his cabin.

"Well, then, gentlemen, let me get back to my work… the next train would be due soon. See you later!" It sounded lame, but he couldn't think of anything else to say.

He left.

It was 2006. Manab Banerjee was now the Station Manager at Rajendra Nagar Terminal station in Patna, a new, prestigious railway station that had been inaugurated in 2003. He was a few years from retirement, had a wife and three grown kids. Though in his mid-50s, he was still slim, energetic, and had special abilities to get things done under the most trying circumstances. This quality had brought him into the notice of his seniors many times leading to personal commendation by the union railway minister of that time. He had been around many stations, had led a life not uninteresting, and had been brought in as the Station Manager at Rajendra Nagar on the special command of the same railway minister.

This particular day had been like any other. As the commander in chief, so to say, of the station, many things came up to him for his approval, sanction, permission, waiver, and denial. Decisions were his chief responsibility.

He had had a routine morning; his lunch had been interrupted briefly by a phone call from his boss asking him to step in—again—to handle the railway minister's impending visit to Patna and consequent visits to the two main railway stations of the city. And now, he had just managed to pacify an irate passenger complaining about the filthy state of train toilets and send him off, and had settled down to his well-earned afternoon cup of tea and a soothing cigarette, while instructing his shift ASM on train berthing plans, when there was a rattle on the office door and someone walked in.

"Manab-*babu*[13]!"

An oldish man with grey beard and glasses walked in, a smile shining through his whiskers. His eyes twinkled behind his glasses, a bag slung over his left shoulder.

"Can you recognise me?" He smiled impishly.

For the life of him, Manab couldn't place him right away. He appeared so familiar and yet the identity escaped him. Then suddenly it struck him.

"Isn't that Biswas-*da*!"

The man laughed aloud with pleasure. "Of course it is!"

Manab jumped up from his chair, dropped his cigarette and rushed towards Biswas. "It's been so long now!" Holding Biswas by his shoulders, he exclaimed, "Must be thirty years, right?"

"Yes! Thirty years it is, my old friend! How have you been?"

A few minutes of reminiscing were inevitable but Manab sensed Biswas wanted to say something else.

The moment Manab paused Biswas broke in. His eyes gleamed with mischief.

"I've to show you something… someone!"

---

[13] A suffix used in Bengali to denote a degree of respect; perhaps not quite as formal as the prefix 'Mr..' but a notch more than just the name

Manab stood quiet, unable to anticipate.

Biswas turned towards the entrance door and raised his voice. "Uday! Uday! Come here, quick!"

He must have been waiting just outside the door for a tall, good-looking, strapping young man walked in, a little hesitant, perhaps a little uncomfortable doing what he had been clearly asked to do.

Biswas held Uday by his arm, a proud smile on his face. "Manab-*babu*, this is my son, Uday." He turned to Uday without waiting for a response from Manab, who stood in a daze.

"Uday, touch his feet! He's had a great influence on things concerning us… quick now!"

Uday did as commanded, mumbled something. Manab touched his head in blessing, still in a daze.

Biswas said, "My son is on his way to Rourkela to join the steel plant there as an engineer after a few years working elsewhere." Pride was manifest in his behaviour.

Manab shook his hand, congratulated Uday, and wished him a happy career. Then Biswas sent him off.

"Go now, wait outside with your luggage. I'll be out soon…"

Uday left.

Then Biswas gently asked Manab, "Did you recognise him?"

Manab did not, he had no clue, but his instincts were alight.

Biswas guessed. Smiling, he said, "Yes, it is the same baby you found thirty years ago in the ash heaps outside Mokameh station… do you recall now?"

And the years rolled away off Manab. Tears welled up in his eyes.

Biswas also had tears in his eyes by then. "I kept my promise, Manab-babu… he doesn't even know he is a foundling…"

They hugged.

2
What Goes Around...

The harsh summer sun beat down mercilessly on the hapless few who had unavoidably ventured out. The platform was mostly deserted; a few that had to be there sought shelter under the welcome shade of the corrugated tin roof, vying for the desultory air stirred by the fan turning inadequately, waiting for the next passenger train due in a few minutes at the Mokameh railway station. May was a pitiless month and the early afternoon perhaps the cruellest part of the day.

Ghanshyam, the tea stall man, stood fanning himself. Business was sluggish at best though the evening would see some coins flowing in. It was lunch time anyway and a handful who had to keep body and soul together urgently, had heaved themselves to the snacks counter. The *coolies* were conspicuous by their absence; they usually strictly believed in the dictum 'just in time'. Wheeler's could attract no book lover to browse through, even half-heartedly, the colourful magazines on display. Listlessness ruled, people looked miserable, and tempers frayed quickly; only the drinking water fountains attracted steady custom.

Kailash, one of the day time porters, was heading to the station master's office with the ASM's lunch box, his head wrapped in a wet *gamchha*[14], cursing the heat. He barely responded to a limp hail from Ghanshyam and stalked as quickly as he could to enter the cool office rooms of the SM. The SM was of course home for his fancy lunch. Animesh Sinha had come in place of Rameshwar Mishra about six months ago. A finicky eater, he usually managed

---

[14] Thin cotton towel; also used as a headgear at times

to slip away home for an extended lunch cum siesta, leaving the afternoon responsibilities with the ASM, currently Manab Banerjee.

Manab had been at Mokameh station for almost two and half years now. He had learnt the ropes very well thanks to his ex-boss Rameshwar Mishra who had been a patient and thorough teacher. A variety of responsibilities had come his way, from managing cabins and signals, to platform and passengers. He was now responsible for the day shift at the station proper, from 0800 hours through till 1600 hours. This was typically the busiest shift of the day, with the most trains and the most passengers. Besides of course there were the many freighters that passed. Also, Sinha, who was more of a hands-off personality type, gave him a lot of space… and time. Manab didn't mind the latter at all.

He was still unmarried though there was significant pressure from his mother to quit stalling. He had resisted till now and wanted to continue in that vein for some more time at least. Maybe once he had his next posting. His life in Mokameh revolved round the station, naturally. With the Mokameh social life not quite of the scintillating variety he tended to spend far more time at the station than his duty hours required. In fact his social life was not as bland as it might have been had he not remained at the station beyond his shift timings. The variety of people he met, the curious happenings there, the opportunity to help people in distress or plain old gassing with his pals, his colleagues… they all contributed in keeping his life interesting. And he had fit in. He was a Railways man.

He was on the phone speaking to his counterpart in Barh, a station west of Mokameh on the main line, sorting out a minor issue. The whirling fan above, of an early vintage, managed to twirl the air inside the room, creating a semblance of cooling breeze. Thankfully, being an old building, the ceiling was high but what really helped Manab keep his cool was that he knew how much hotter it was outside really. He was happy to be inside; rolling up his sleeves and keeping his shirt open at the throat were the additional couple of steps to counter the relentless heat.

"Okay, Alam-*sahab*[15], I will inform Animesh-ji of your points. Thanks!"

He rang off as Kailash entered the room and quickly shut the door. He appeared to visibly revive feeling the relative coolness envelop him.

"*Sahib*, here's your lunch. Bodhi was apologizing for not having included the *chhaach*[16] you ordered."

Manab grunted, making some space in front of him on the desk. He had only recently outsourced his lunch to an eatery near the station. The fellow Bodhi provided reasonable stuff that at least tasted different from the fare served in the station canteen. He had been reminding the guy to include the salted buttermilk drink along with his meal since it was considered a coolant for the terrible summer months. Unsuccessfully still, as he could see. He sighed.

Kailash spread an old newspaper on the desk and opened the tiffin carrier. Today there was rice, some specimen of *dal*[17] which was watery, as usual, some green mess which probably was a mixture of a few vegetables, some fried potato chips cut paper thin, and a fish curry. A few pieces of sliced onions in the raw, a cut of lemon and a couple of green chillies made up the whole meal.

After a quick wash in the attached toilet in the office rooms, Manab settled down to his meal. He usually let Kailash go for his own lunch once he spread his fare and today was no exception. There was no point in keeping a hungry man from his lunch.

Just as Kailash was leaving, he said, "Kailash, the Danapur Passenger is due in 10 minutes now. Let me know if there's something I need to intervene in, okay? Tell Prakash to be on the platform." Prakash was another porter who kept an eye on things as the passenger trains halted. He ensured necessary cleaning was done and water refilled in the overhead tanks of the coaches.

---

[15] Same as 'sahib', a suffix of respect

[16] Buttermilk

[17] Lentils

"Yes, *sahib*," Kailash replied, and slightly unhappy to be parted from the cool room, he went for his own meal.

Manab discovered the green mess comprised some *parwal*[18] slices, potato chunks, papaya, and some indeterminate bean-type stringy things. It tasted as it appeared: messy. The fish wasn't bad, really. As he had instructed, the curry was thin, a little watery to facilitate mixing with rice. At least some of his wishes had been carried out! He didn't complain about the food; there was no point. The canteen stuff was no better and with the departure of Mishra, his ex-boss, the pleasures of home-cooked food were few and far between.

He was still eating when he heard the Danapur Passenger steam in; it had been announced of course though it was quite questionable as to who had made out what had been announced considering the state of garbled-ness of the announcement. It had a scheduled halt for five minutes. Since the rush was quite a bit, every minute of that halt was necessary. At times—too frequently, in Manab's opinion— the train was delayed by some passenger pulling the chain.

He heard the usual commotion as passengers got off and some boarded the train. The hustle belied the heat but then who cared for that when a train was to be boarded or de-boarded! He paid scant attention to the noise outside. If there was some need for his intervention he'd get to know of that soon enough.

And exactly at that moment, just as he was at the psychological point of extracting pieces of fine bone from a chunk of fish in his mouth, there were several loud gunshots outside. He was too stunned to react.

There were rending cries immediately after and a general hubbub as he heard people pounding away… their footsteps fading along with cries of panic. By then he had managed to break the spell of shock and stagger out of his chair. He ran towards the door that opened on to the platform. There was a window placed to the side of the door which was open, and his eyes beheld a scene so grotesque that it froze him, with a hand still on the handle of the door.

———————————

[18] A vegetable: pointed gourd

The office was on platform 1 and the door opened on to it. The Danapur Passenger stood at that platform and from immediately in front of his office were lined the compartments[19], the engine presumably to his left, out of sight. About hundred feet to his right, in a semicircle around the foreside gate of a compartment, stood several men, perhaps 7 or 8. Each held a gun, a couple armed with double-barrelled shotguns, the rest with guns with curved magazines. They were dressed as any average local person would: trousers, topped with half sleeved shirts or long, plain white *kurta*[20]. Most had *gamchha* wrapped around their heads though not with the intention of hiding their identity for no one's face was covered.

Even as he watched thunderstruck, a couple of those goons shouldered their guns—both the shotgun guys—and fired a round each into the air. They had struck enough shock and awe into every soul around them for already no one was visible on the platform as far as Manab could see. Not a single GRP man was in sight either though they sometimes slouched or strutted around the station with their bolt action rifles slung on their shoulders.

Manab was about to turn the handle on his door to go out and… he had no idea what he'd do there but surely *someone* had to do *something*… when the door was violently thrust open and Kailash rushed in, his eyes wide with fear.

"*Sahib*!" His voice was a hoarse whisper.

Manab looked at him, his own expression not much different.

"*Sahib*! Don't go out… whatever else you might do!"

"Eh?" Manab gaped at him in surprise.

Kailash clamped his hand on Manab's wrist—something completely never done under normal circumstances—and continued his hoarse whispering.

"These men *sahib*, they're killers! Don't go out!"

---

[19] Coaches/ carriages/ passenger cars

[20] Long (thigh or knee length), loose shirt worn over pyjamas, dhoti, or trousers

Manab didn't know what to do… his mind was in turmoil. He understood the danger in some vague, smoky manner, his sense of responsibility far more pronounced. But he held back.

Then Kailash suddenly gestured, pointing out of the window. "Look!"

Manab turned back and saw one of the armed men enter the coach, transferring his gun to his left hand. He was quickly followed by another man who held a shotgun. The windows of the coach were eerily empty: the window-side passengers were probably keeping their heads literally low.

While the two men disappeared inside the compartment, their companions waved their guns around, eyes swivelling in every direction, clearly indicating they were alert for anyone trying any sort of misadventure.

Some semblance of sense filtered into Manab's mind. He knew in his bones he had to get the train out of the station… somehow, and immediately.

"Kailash!" He had turned back from the window. "We need to get the train out of here… West cabin has to signal departure… now!"

It barely registered with Kailash… he was pointing with a shaking finger. The man with the rifle was climbing down from the coach steps… dragging a man by his hair.

Manab stood transfixed, helpless and uncomprehending but aware of impending terror, probably triggered by his sixth sense.

The man dragged his victim further away from the coach, the gang of armed men going along. They stopped near a wall opposite the coach and without pausing, the man who had dragged his prey out started slapping him, methodically, across and back. Slap! Slap! Slap! The reports were loud enough to reach Manab who still stood in a trance.

Something snapped his attention back from his trance-like state. He turned with a jerk towards Kailash.

"Run to the driver Kailash, run to him! Tell him I've ordered him away from here immediately! I'll call Tal[21] and get line clear for its immediate departure!"

The urgency in his tone of voice was such that Kailash left immediately, sidling out and then sprinting away. None of the gang challenged him. Manab sprang to his desk and rang up the cabin in-charge and instructed him in a few sharp words. Then he went back to his vantage point by the window, his curiosity shadowed by a sick foreboding.

By this time each of the gang had joined in on the slapping, their victim on his knees, ineffectually trying to protect his face. Abruptly, they ceased the marathon slapping, leaving the man limp from the thrashing. He was messy and bleeding from his nose, almost in a stupor. The man who had dragged him out suddenly thrust out his hand evidently expecting something. While the others looked around waving their weapons menacingly, one man took out a sickle and placed it in his hand.

Cold sweat broke out on Manab's face, seized by the strongest emotions but entirely rooted where he stood. He gaped on, unable to blink or breathe.

In slow deliberate movements, the man with the sickle, standing behind his victim, pulled back the head of his quarry by his hair, exposing his throat fully while shrill shrieks escaped him. Four accomplices of the main assaulter held their prey's arms and legs, pinning him immobile. The rest stepped back a little.

The grim-faced man brought the sickle down to his victim's throat and with the same deliberateness, he drew the first stroke. The man struggled helplessly but the sudden blowing of steam from the train engine muffled his cries, as it prepared to steam out. Manab stood transfixed still, horror building upon revulsion. The killer didn't pause. As the train pulled out unchallenged by the gangsters,

---

[21] Name of the next station from where line clearance was needed for the train to proceed on its designated route

he continued sawing at the exposed throat. By the third stroke a stream of blood squirted out, spraying the wall opposite, drenching a gaudily coloured movie poster stuck there that incongruously depicted a romantic couple.

The bloodbath continued, the killer sawing on, blood gushing, spraying, drenching. None of the gang flinched or displayed any discomfort in their macabre objective. Their victim was soon dead, limbs limp, blood no longer gushing… barely trickling. And yet the sawing didn't stop.

Manab's stomach heaved in nausea, his mind unable to cope with the horrific visual. Numbness seemed to have taken over completely. Why didn't the killer stop, for God's sake? Why keep on sawing when the man was clearly dead?

The killer kept on hacking for several minutes until finally he had severed the head completely. He held the decapitated head in his left hand, slightly raised, clutching it by the hair still. The headless body toppled over on the floor and lay twitching. Blood rolled down his elbow as the killer handed over the sickle to one of his sidekicks and then took a proffered *gamchha* with which he wrapped the head and then held it with the edges bunched, a grotesque lump hanging.

The entire front of the killer's *kurta* was drenched red, gore up to his elbows, even his face speckled with blood. He stooped to pick up his gun and then led the group out of the station, carrying the macabre package in his left hand. His companions fired a few more rounds as they left and soon the station stood eerily quiet, deceptively peaceful excepting for the spot where the deed had been done: the headless body lay there in the shapeless heap of death, blood pooling around and the movie poster that now barely had anything legible left visible.

Reaction set in as Manab stood there unable to move. His knees felt buttery and he clutched the nearest wall for support. The bloodiness of the scene outside was a searing reminder of the gruesome killing a few minutes earlier. His stomach heaved again… and this time, uncontrollably. He tottered from there, intending to reach the toilet before the retching overcame his restraint.

He was still heaving out the contents of his half-eaten lunch a few minutes later when Kailash hurried back in. He was immediately solicitous and fetched Manab some water to sip when he had cleaned himself up. But his daze refused to reduce; a weakness pervaded his every sense. He staggered back to his desk, leaning on it. Try as he might he just couldn't erase the ghoulish scene from his mind. The beheading played on as a movie reel in an unending loop.

After a few minutes, he felt a bit more in control of himself. He still didn't hear any hubbub from outside and with a shudder he remembered he needed to take care of the headless body lying outside. With a shake of his head to clear the cobwebs, he spoke to Kailash:

"We need to go out now, Kailash… we've work to do!"

And he strode out with firm resolve, Kailash close behind.

He saw inspector Sashikant Dubey of the GRP near the headless body that lay in a sickly pool of already congealing blood, but his eyes were transfixed upon the gruesome, incongruous blood-splattered film poster on the wall next to the body. It seemed to somehow accentuate the grisliness of the mayhem.

"*Dada!*" The voice didn't cut through his trance, only a touch on his shoulder jerked him to awareness. It was the inspector.

A surge of anger coursed through Manab, sudden and implacable, triggered by the sight of the inspector and a couple of his troopers, each armed with guns.

"Inspector!" His voice trembled with emotion. "Where were you hiding!" It was not a question, it was an accusation. He noticed distractedly that he was shaking a finger at the policeman who appeared bemused.

Manab pointed dementedly at the body lying at their feet. "Look at that! A wanton killing happened in broad daylight… and the police was missing!"

He almost pirouetted in fulminating anger. "Why! Government issues you guns! To do what! Hide when you need to use them!"

With a gesture of infinite patience, Inspector Dubey held Manab by his shoulders. "*Dada*! *Dada*, calm down, listen to me."

Manab was trying to wriggle out of the inspector's grasp who tried to hold on, gripping harder.

"*Dada*! You've to listen to me!" Dubey had introduced a bit of steel into his voice which seemed to get through.

"Eh?"

Dubey spoke softly. "Did you notice their guns, *Dada*?"

As Manab gaped at him, Dubey didn't wait for his answer. "They had 3 or 4 automatic rifles between them *Dada*, besides shotguns. They were AK-47s. You know how many rounds they fire per second?"

Manab had no clue and remained quiet.

Dubey continued, still quietly. "They fire 10 rounds per second… 600 rounds per minute! And you know how many rounds our guns can fire per second?"

This time Manab was constrained to shake his head.

Dubey was inexorable. "One round, *Dada*. One. It's a bolt action rifle… you fire then you pull the bolt back, eject the shell, shove the next round in, push the bolt back, aim and then fire… obviously, by then, they'd have fried us entirely."

Manab found his voice. He spoke hoarsely. "So… you'll abandon poor passengers to their death? You'll use your guns only when you know the other party cannot fire back?"

Dubey sighed. "You've to deal with one body now, *Dada*. If we'd been as foolhardy as you'd have us be, you'd have to deal with many more bodies, do you realise that?"

Manab shook his head, suddenly calmer. "It's your *job*, inspector…"

"Tell me something *Dada*. You know what would happen if I were to be killed on duty? Do you know?"

Before Manab could reply, Dubey went on. "What would happen at most? You'd give my wife a job on grounds of sympathy… right?" He waved a hand dismissively and continued. "She's uneducated… so you'll only give her a grade 4 job… a peon, someone who'd perhaps serve you tea from Ghanshyam's… and that's the life she'd lead… all because her husband was a brave man who took on men with automatic rifles!" He shook his head at the absurdity of the imagery he had created.

Manab could visualise the entire chain, unbidden. While he still felt outraged that the police, who're responsible for the protection of the station and the safety of the passengers, had failed miserably, the possible outcome of Dubey's scenario would have only led to a bigger mayhem, a grislier dance of death on the platform of his station. Was his sense of what would be possibly just be justification enough? With a sigh, he turned to face Dubey.

"You saw them too, didn't you? I am not the only eyewitness, right?"

"Of course I did! That's the reason I know what guns they're carrying and knew we could never take them on with our antiquated bolt action guns!" Dubey had no reluctance in admitting this.

Manab shook his head. "What do you suggest now?"

Dubey looked confused. "I don't understand, *Dada*… what do you mean?"

Manab pointed at the body. "I mean this, Dubey-ji. I must report this, right? To you, isn't it?" He started to move off in a distraught manner when Dubey held his arm.

"Wait, *Dada*! What will you report?"

Manab was perplexed, irritation growing exponentially. He spoke with exaggerated patience.

"Exactly what happened, Dubey-ji. I saw everything that happened, d'you know? Everything!" He glared at the inspector.

The inspector appeared to take his outburst very calmly. He heaved a long sigh and started to speak gently. Again.

"*Dada*, that's exactly what you will *not* do!"

As Manab gaped at him, he went on. "Do you know who those men were?"

A rush of images whirled through Manab's mind. Those grim men with their guns—automatic rifles—their apparently ordinary appearance, their methodical butchering of their hapless victim… He had no idea who they were and what was their reason for slaughtering that passenger. The shock of the incident had suspended his reasoning, but this exchange brought that back to life once again. There had to be some reason, possibly some terrible reason, for perpetrating a horrific execution. It was an execution, nothing less.

"N-no…"

"Neither do I, *dada*. I don't know them either, none of them." Before Manab could comment acidly on this he continued.

"But I can tell you this. They are extremely dangerous men and they'll kill at the slightest provocation!"

Dubey went on in a conversational tone. "What will you report? That you saw several men storm the station, drag a man out of the train and then kill him? Describe them? You know what they'd do then? They'll hunt you down… track you down and kill you right here… you understand? Like this afternoon, one sunny day, very soon, they'd come here, waving and firing their guns… walk into your little office and spray you with bullets!"

Manab stood in shock, speechless. He had obviously not thought it through, just the thought of his responsibility to report the incident. Not for a second had Manab considered that possibility, it had simply not occurred to him. A chill ran through him remembering the cool callousness of the killers. He looked mutely at Dubey. With a strong effort, he spoke.

"Then what should I do, Dubey-ji?"

Dubey spoke gently. "Keep it simple, *dada*. Just that you heard some gunfire and when you rushed out you saw this headless body. That you have no idea who this is and who were the perpetrators…"

As Manab gazed at Dubey unseeingly, one aspect of this story struck him. "B-but… how can I say I didn't see anything! I had cleared the Danapur passenger while the crime was underway! How can I deny that?"

"Don't worry, *dada*. You were inside the office and realising the grave danger that the passengers faced you quickly instructed for the train to depart early, saving lives." Dubey's voice was soothing. "You might even earn a commendation!"

Manab was repelled at that thought. "No!" He shook his head vigorously. "I wouldn't want any recognition on false pretences!"

Suddenly, he noticed that people had started to come back to the station. What had been a deserted stretch on every side was now limping back to some semblance of normalcy. And unless they took quick action they would have an unwanted bunch of people gaping vulture-like at the headless body.

"Dubey-ji! Please get your men to keep the people away from this spot! Let's get the necessary formalities done so that the body can be removed, and the place cleaned up." Manab got a grip on himself with an effort.

Dubey swung into action, instructing his men to set up a perimeter and then they went back into the SM's office to complete the formalities.

It was a few days after the grisly murder. Manab had gone off duty at 1600 hours in the afternoon but as usual, had hung around, chatting, and catching up with staff and certain regulars who dropped by. The sun set late in the summer months and thus it was quite light even after 1800 hours. Manab sat along with a few of the regulars in the benches laid out in front of Ghanshyam's tea stall. Dubey was there, and so was Animesh Sinha. Kailash lurked on and off. And among the several regulars, there was old Jha-ji, who ran the Wheeler's at the station. He was a storehouse of gossip, with a veritable ear to the ground. He loved to gas with the men in the evenings, over tea and biscuits, with the occasional summer breeze providing some relief. He had been away the last few days, so his presence added to all their knowledge of the latest local gossip. This evening too, as had been usual the last few days, the topic had turned toward the sensational killing that had been reported in every local newspaper.

"So, Manab-*babu*, it's unfortunate you burnt that blood-sodden film poster! You'd have kept it… as a memento!" Jha-ji's eyes crinkled with humour. He knew of Manab's distaste and needled him occasionally.

Manab laughed. "Actually, you're right! I'd have kept it and presented you with it! You seem to miss it so much!"

Animesh Sinha, who was browsing through a Hindi local newspaper, exclaimed suddenly. "These guys contradict themselves! Yesterday this paper said the killing was political but today's editorial claims personal enmity! Why can't they stick to one story?"

They acknowledged that with a chuckle. Truly, the reporting had been fairly speculative. Some suggested many men had come to make a political statement involving castes, while some reported it had been the work of a couple of men. Since there had been no reported eyewitnesses the stories depended on impressions and varying stories from people who claimed they had *heard* things first-hand. As far as Manab and Dubey were concerned, they held each other's versions up. They suspected their friends suspected them of knowing more but let it pass.

Ghanshyam piped up while serving their next round of milky tea and biscuits. "I heard today that these killers were local… someone was saying."

"Oh, as if they'd come from far to kill in Mokameh! C'mon Ghanshyam… they must be people from nearby!" Animesh scoffed.

Dubey smiled. "Yes… they'd be from nearby. Some who knew of their victim's travel plan, his routine… whether the train was on time… everything. They might have followed the train too. From somewhere close… to pinpoint the extraction." He looked around his companions. "Speaking as a policeman, of course. Applying reason…"

Jha-ji looked shrewdly at Dubey. "Are you any close to catching the culprits?"

Dubey sipped his tea leisurely before replying. "Jha-ji, you know that's not my jurisdiction. The case is being investigated by the local police… so when Inspector Khan is here next, you can check with him." He smiled to take any possible sting out of his reply.

Manab blurted out something that had been bothering him several days. He'd posed this before but never got any satisfying answer. Perhaps Jha-ji would shed some unexpected light?

"One thing that has bothered me no end since that day is the missing head. Why did they take the man's head away?"

That got their attention for sure. Since this was not a new question, there was a lull as they pondered. That the head could have been taken to make identification difficult had already been discussed and almost discarded for the killers had behaved with impunity and imagining them worried about hiding or delaying their victim's identification didn't quite wash. They simply didn't care if the identity was known or not. And seriously, it couldn't really be prevented anyway.

One of the other regulars, a middle-aged trader from the town, shook his head ponderously. "I can't imagine any other reason to take the head away… what sane men would do that?"

Animesh snorted derisively. "Sanity doesn't come into the picture! Those killers are not sane!"

Jha-ji sighed loudly. His tone of voice caught everyone's attention there. Somehow it portended at what he'd say would bring an angle to the incident that they hadn't known or imagined.

"You gentlemen really don't know the background then, eh?"

Each of them looked at old Jha. Manab remembered the numerous occasions when the old man had given them insight to various incidents that somehow completed the story being discussed, or opened up a new line of thought or made them pause, to think.

"There's a village not too far from here… Chadheriya. Maybe some 15-20 kilometres. Heard of it?"

They looked at each other. Finally, Dubey said, "Yes, I've heard of it, Jha-ji. What of it?"

"It's a run-of-the-mill village, nothing special… our story is from there."

"Go on, Jha-ji. Tell us." Manab was breathless.

Jha was silent for a bit. Then, with a wry smile, he said, "The man they killed was the *mukhiya*[22] of the village."

There was complete silence. Then Dubey asked, softly, "How do you know that, Jha-ji? The body's not been identified yet… even Khan doesn't know else I'd have known."

Jha only smiled. "Then he'll confirm this… eventually when they find out… 'officially'. For now, just know that I know. Let us call him Hoshiyar Singh for our purpose now."

Manab knew from his experience that Jha seldom revealed his sources, if ever. There was no point pressing him.

As Dubey quietly looked at Jha, Manab spoke up. "Jha-ji, is that all? Or do you have more to say?"

Jha grinned and the others leaned forward in barely controlled eagerness. Jha usually proved himself rather well informed.

---

[22] Village headman

He gathered himself. "No, there's more, you're right." He nodded at Manab and continued. "Why they carried off his head is of course the rest of the story…"

Like the seasoned raconteur he was, he paused, drawing out their curiosity. "Last year, perhaps you'll recall, there was a gruesome murder in Chadheriya, late in the monsoon season. Do you remember?"

After almost a minute's silence Dubey murmured, "Perhaps… are you talking of the killing where a man was chased in the fields by a gang and then beheaded by one of them? A ghastly affair, yes!"

Jha nodded. "Yes, that's the one I meant. Does anyone else recall that one?"

Kailash, who had sidled up surreptitiously, breathed, "Yes *sahib*! I do! Very gory it was too… Bisiya had narrated that to me…"

The others glanced fleetingly at Kailash, switching their focus back to Jha. Suddenly, Dubey clapped his forehead loudly.

"That man they killed in the fields was the *mukhiya*, Premnath Singh! I remember now!"

He looked with a wild surmise at Jha who grinned back humourlessly. "You're right Dubey-ji," he said. "That was indeed the then *mukhiya* of Chadheriya. But do you know who killed him?"

This time Dubey was on it and the others deferred since his source was the local police. He said, excitedly, "That was never found out… the villagers there knew nothing and eventually they closed the case as unsolved! It was taken that outsiders killed him to settle some unknown personal matters… perhaps gambling debts!"

"Nonsense!" Jha exploded scathingly. "Gambling debts! Bah! Nothing of the sort! The man who killed him wanted to become the *mukhiya*. And he wielded enough brutal power to coerce the villagers into making him it once Premnath had been disposed of…" Then he smiled coldly.

"Hoshiyar Singh was the name of the man that killed Premnath

Singh." Quiet descended upon the group momentarily and a collective gasp exploded when they made the connection.

Manab stammered, "You mean to say… it was the murderer of Premnath Singh who was killed on the platform of this station a few days ago?"

Jha nodded. "Yes, Hoshiyar Singh is the man… the same one who chased down Premnath and beheaded him with his own hands." He looked at them in the eye, adding quietly, "You might even say justice caught up with him… in the most brutal manner imaginable."

There was stillness for the next few moments then Manab stirred, sensing they were close to the finale… which was not yet reached.

"There's more you know Jha-ji… isn't it?" he asked gently. As Jha looked quizzically at him, he went on. "Who killed Hoshiyar Singh then? Revenge? And the taking of the head? Why's that?"

Jha laughed softly, almost to himself. "So many questions!" He shook his head and said, "Premnath had a younger brother, Pratap, who used to study in Patna. He went back to his village upon the murder of his brother, distressed by the state of his *bhauji*[23] who he looked upon as his mother since his own had died when he was very young."

"So…" began Animesh when he was interrupted by Jha.

"Yes, Pratap swore revenge…"

Dubey let out a low whistle. "So, it was Pratap who hacked Hoshiyar Singh's head off…"

The group was quiet again briefly before Manab prompted. "And the head…?"

Jha looked away at the mid-distance. "Apparently, Pratap had promised to wash the *sindoor*[24] off his *bhauji*'s forehead with Hoshiyar Singh's blood. Seems he fulfilled his promise, eh?"

---

[23] Wife of the elder brother

[24] Vermillion, used by Hindu married women as a sign of marriage, applied usually in the parting of their hair

3

The Lone Passenger

Dense winter fog had already begun rolling in from the nearby Ganga that early evening, even before the Mokameh-Barauni passenger had reached Rajendra Pul station, scheduled, as always, for 1635 hours. It was darker than usual for the same reason, contributing to the overall gloominess. The train was making its way across the river and would soon berth at the platform which anyone would have been hard-pressed to distinguish from the surrounding terrain.

Rajendra Pul was a stop on the Mokameh – Barauni route, just before another small station, Simaria. It was a mere speck in the vast ocean of Indian Railways, relatively speaking of course. Back in 1978, it didn't merit electricity, and not even a building. A tin shed did duty instead and oil-fired lanterns for light. Staff strength was as meagre; besides the ASM, a leverman, and a porter—though he was more of an all-rounder—made up the total team. Only a couple of passenger trains deigned to stop there through the day and none in the night; life could be dreary there. There were no shops for miles around and no place to get any food, indeed, even a *kulhar*[25] of tea.

Bholenath Baranwal—more often BB to everyone—was the ASM on duty for that shift which was scheduled to end at 0600 hours the following morning, with his handing over to the next person.

The porter in the same shift, Kunj Bihari, played a heroic role here. Besides the regular—though limited in scope compared to a porter

---

[25] Clay cup

in a regular station—duties of a porter, he cooked, he washed, he fetched, he cleaned, he even cultivated a kitchen garden. If it was not there in his job description, then it was likely it didn't need to be done. He had even managed to coerce the other porters to look after his garden when he was off-duty.

The leverman on duty, Shambhunath, was the oldest among them. The unique feature of his role, entirely not in his job description, was to be the bravest man there. He was the one who took it upon himself to check things in the dark.

3MB1—Mokameh-Barauni passenger—came to a stop at the only platform, the diesel engine growls rattling in the gathering gloom, and sounded the mandatory whistle announcing that it had stopped. Less than a dozen passengers alighted and quickly made their way out of the station, while the two waiting to board hopped on as quickly. Just on the one-minute mark, the train announced it would depart this forsaken spot and roll on for livelier ones. The tootle it blew accentuated the loneliness surrounding the station, and it shuddered into motion. As the growly-rattles dissipated and the train stepped on the gas, far in the murky depths of the foggy evening, towards the engine end of the now departing train, there appeared to be standing a lonely figure. The swirling fog gave a halo effect to that man and BB wondered why was that lone passenger still lingering on the platform.

The man was enveloped from his head downwards in what appeared to be a ragged blanket, with a *dhoti*[26] peeping beneath that. He was clutching a bundle in his left arm and a long stick in his right.

In a quiet voice, BB spoke to the leverman who was only a few feet behind him. "Shambhu, check! Who on earth is this man?"

Shambhu had scant regard for the eerie and armed with his trusty staff, he strode forward. BB watched keenly from where he stood,

---

[26] A plain length of cloth, usually white, worn by men around the legs, especially in the rural areas

as did Kunj Bihari, who had by then come over from his corner where he had just started preparations for their dinner.

The man had also started walking towards them, meeting Shambhu midway, where they stopped and spoke briefly. Then they both came on towards them. BB heaved a sigh of relief for if Shambhu was satisfied, it was likely things were fine.

"Sir," began Shambhu. Incidentally, he was one of the few personnel of that staff grade who used this form of address and not the far commoner 'sahib'.

"Sir, this is Kesoram, from the village of Khejuria, a few kilometres from Minapur. He's returning home but wants to spend the night here…"

Kesoram appeared to be a middle-aged man, with a grey stubble that was at least 4-day old but a mostly-black moustache that was full and curled up at the edges. His eyes had a piercing glint though that could have been a trick played by the fading daylight. Interestingly, he wore brass earrings in both ears.

BB was aware of Minapur, some three kilometres distant from there but he hadn't heard of Khejuria though these hamlets were in their hundreds and none who wasn't local could claim to have heard of them all; it was normal.

Kunj Bihari spoke up. "*Sahib*, I know of Khejuria. The fellow that comes weekly with the vegetables… Nathu, he picks up potatoes from there to sell in the *haat*[27] in Simaria.

Okay, BB thought, so Khejuria exists. But why spend the night here?

"But why do you want to spend the night here?" BB was direct, something he had a penchant for.

Kesoram spoke for the first time, in a surprisingly deep voice but very rustic speech.

---

[27] Regular informal market, particularly in rural areas

"*Sahib*, I'd have walked to my village but it's far, another 3-4 *kos*[28] from Minapur… it'll be dark soon and colder too. I'd prefer to do that in daylight… if you'd let me sleep in a corner of your station… anywhere, I don't need to be inside the shed… just anywhere will do… and I'll leave early tomorrow morning… may I, please, *sahib*?"

BB looked steadily at him. "Do you have any food with you?" he asked. "There's nothing available around here… nothing at all…"

The man looked embarrassed. "No, *sahib*, but don't worry, it's just for the night… I'll manage!"

BB waved dismissively. "Nah, you shouldn't sleep on an empty stomach." He turned towards Kunj Bihari. "Bihari, make a bit more so that our guest can also have some food in his belly, okay?"

As Kunj Bihari nodded and turned to go back to his 'kitchen', BB walked back inside the shed to his chair, wrapped the thick shawl around himself and picked up his half-finished novel.

Shambhu told Kesoram where to get a wash if he wanted and then went off to where he usually sat, a cozy spot off to one side from the shed. He sat down and started to roll himself some chewing tobacco, preparing to doze until dinner. The nights were especially slow.

Darkness seemed to descend swiftly, and the swirling fog made things damp and grey. Kunj Bihari had resumed his dinner preparations; he washed a few potatoes and a couple of brinjals and then, when he started peeling and cutting them for the curry he planned to cook, Kesoram came and squatted uninvited. He took some *khaini*[29] in his palm from his *batua*[30] tucked into a roll at his waist and started grinding it with his thumb, mixing it with a touch of *choona*[31]. Bihari cast him a look but kept silent, continuing his

---

[28] An ancient measure of distance still used in villages (at the time of this incident), roughly 1 kos measures 1.8 km

[29] Chewing tobacco, mixed with edible-lime; usually, a great conversation starter among aficionados

[30] Cloth pouch, usually with a drawstring; tucked into the waistband in a tight roll

[31] Edible-lime

peeling and cutting. Silence reigned until the *khaini* was ready to be shared. He took a pinch and offered it to Bihari, unasked, who took it and carefully placed it in a strategic corner of his mouth then washed his hand. The pre-conversation lubrication done, it flowed smoother.

They struck a chord right away, exchanging local gossip, family backgrounds, and when Kesoram figured out Bihari's love for his kitchen garden, in great detail about that. Bihari grew tomatoes, and a variety of vegetables, principal among them brinjal, radish, turnip, a bit of cabbage, green chillies, and several types of herbs too. Encouraged, he dived into the peculiarities of some vegetables, their downright animosity in responding to his directives and the others that were friendly and responsive. Kesoram sympathised and soon, he was helping Bihari with his cooking, washing and straining the diced vegetables, then fetching this and extending that, until the companionship was natural and flowing. Soon, Bihari got the *roti*[32] ready and in a short while their sumptuous dinner of *roti* and *alu-baingain sabzi*[33] was ready.

Just before serving the meal for everyone, Bihari rose to fetch a bucket of water for cleaning up after their dinner. Kesoram smiled apologetically.

"I'd fetch it too, but I have some pain in my arms when I pick heavier weights… so…"

Kunj Bihari smiled, eyes crinkling in recognition of his offer, and waved his hand dismissively.

"Why should you be sorry, my friend? I do it every day… don't worry about it…" With that he stepped off with the empty iron bucket, vanishing from sight in the darkness immediately off the small cooking area.

Kesoram looked thoughtfully at the receding figure and then

---

[32] Flatbread cooked dry usually on an iron griddle; staple with curries and lentils

[33] A dryish curry of potato and brinjal (eggplant)

casually glanced around. Station Master *sahib* was still reading and Shambhu was dozing, his figure dimly visible in the distance.

Bihari was back within a couple of minutes with a full bucket. Then he served the food in tin plates and handed them to the others.

Pankaj Kumar, the ASM on duty at Mokameh, was frustrated. For the last fifteen minutes he had been trying to get line clear confirmation from Rajendra Pul but in vain. He had set the Line Clear machine to "going on line" and he needed the confirmation from that station to release the freight train waiting at Mokameh on its way to Barauni, which lay beyond Rajendra Pul. For some reason, the ASM on duty there was just not responding. Finally, in frustration, he called Control at Danapur, the division headquarters.

"Hello, Control? Mokameh station!"

"Yes, Mokameh?" The speaker at the other end was Karamjit Singh, an ebullient *sardar*[34] who lived up to the popular imagination of what a jolly *sardar* looked and behaved like.

Pankaj explained his problem and that he had been trying to raise Rajendra Pul for the last fifteen minutes but to no avail. His freighter was delayed.

"Let me check..." Singh sounded serious, the usual levity absent. Singh activated the direct connection with Rajendra Pul and sounded the bell there. There was no response. A couple of repeats elicited no different a response.

Singh came back on line with Pankaj. "Has BB fallen asleep?" he chuckled loudly.

Such lapses, though rare, weren't quite unknown. If the station master on duty fell asleep there was every possibility that the other staff may not even know the Control phone was ringing.

"You know BB, right?"

"Of course."

---

[34] Common reference to Sikh men

"I think we should check. Continuing absence of line advice can lead to problems…"

'Advising line' was the term used between stations to set the line to be used between one station and the next. So, the station that was releasing a train from there would set the Line Clear machine to "going on line" and the next station would set its Line Clear machine to "coming on line" appropriately, thus completing the circuit, so to say, between those two stations. It was a failsafe mechanism to ensure the line on which the designated train travelled would not be 'advised' to another train. If a station was not doing this and not responding to Control, train movement would be impacted.

"I see. What do you advise?" Pankaj understood the gravity of the situation.

"Get Pratap... and… Banerjee. He, I mean, Manab Banerjee, he is off-duty, right?" Singh asked.

"Yes, *dada* is not on duty tonight…" Pankaj replied.

"Good. Despatch a porter to call both Pratap and Manab. Detach the engine from your freighter and instruct the driver and his assistant to take them at walking speed to Rajendra Pul. Check what is wrong. We'll take action based on that."

It was standard operating procedure to proceed at walking speed when a line cannot be advised; in case of any sudden emergency— like a train approaching from the other end—it can be stopped quickly.

"Yes, I'll have this done right away!" They disconnected.

Pankaj called Hariya and instructed him to run and fetch Pratap Tiwari as well as Manab, from their homes. Thankfully, they lived nearby but even so it would take an hour and more for them to start for Rajendra Pul.

Pratap Tiwari was the Traffic Inspector posted at Mokameh. The TI was responsible to monitor procedural compliance and personnel checks within his section. He would typically visit different spots and ensure operations ran the way they were supposed to under normal operating conditions.

Pankaj walked over to the waiting freight train's diesel engine. The driver and the assistant driver were both sitting on the footboard there, awaiting clearance to resume their journey to Barauni, their destination.

"Devesh-ji," he spoke to the driver. "I need you to detach your engine and run the ASM, Manab Banerjee, and the TI, Pratap Tiwari, to Rajendra Pul for an inspection… they're not responding to line clear requests. We need to check."

After a brief exchange, they agreed to detach and be ready for departure well before Pratap and Manab got to the station.

While Pankaj waited for them to reach, he thought about the situation. The most likely reason would be BB falling asleep but what if that was not the case? It would be natural to suspect some form of foul play then… so what could it be? It was not even a station that would have a load of cash for any robbery to be committed. But what if…? Should not Kishan Dubey, the GRP inspector, go along? At least one rifle between them? Sure, RPF patrol could be nearby but just to be prepared?

Manab was the first to arrive, close on to midnight. He had heard of the circumstances from Hariya but wanted a more detailed briefing from Pankaj. Having heard that out, he too concurred with the general opinion that BB must have fallen asleep. Pratap reached soon after this and both Manab and Pankaj explained the matter and that the engine was ready to take them to Rajendra Pul.

Manab and Pratap then hurried out, each armed with a stick, a couple of powerful torchlights and a pair of lanterns, to boot. Just as he reached the door of the office, it struck Manab they would do well to carry the First Aid kit also. Who knew what they would find there? Hariya sprinted for the box and by the time they had boarded the engine, he returned with the kit. They started immediately.

Rajendra Pul lay about twelve kilometres in the east from Mokameh. It would be a short ride though he instructed the driver to go at walking speed, strictly by the book. Manab realised that their tension was rising with every yard they covered. The fear of the unknown…

Soon they had reached Hatidah, a small station just before the edge of the Ganga and the driver proceeded with caution. They were moving at a snail's pace as they crossed the bridge over the wide expanse of the river. Once over it, their destination lay straight up though it was not visible in the inky blackness; the engine's lamp merely reflected off the dense fog creating a weird glow that stayed just ahead of them.

Manab wondered if any of them was awake… conscious, he might see the glow of their light and… do what? Swing a lantern? No chance of that happening since they had not been communicating for quite some time now. What would they find?

The tension had evidently seeped into the driver also for he spoke in a hushed voice a few minutes later.

"We've reached… should I just stop?"

Manab grunted for he too could make out the outline of the tin shed, a darker shade of black. There was no sign of anyone of the three regular staff members. Manab felt a fresh wave of anxiety rising in him. He swung the beam of his torchlight around… The place was desolate.

Manab and Pratap stepped off the engine. Both had been to this station before of course so they were familiar with the layout. Torchlights in their left hand and the sticks in their right, they crept up to the shed, slow, and cautious.

As they were creeping forward, the night was pierced by what sounded like a demonic phone ringing. It startled both men, then they chuckled embarrassedly for it was only the Control phone ringing. Singh must be trying his luck just in case. They were just outside the shed, their torchlight picking out the entrance in sharp contrast. They entered as the phone rang off.

Manab swung his beam to the right while Pankaj swung his left. One swerve of his beam and Manab spotted BB lying on the floor, canted on his right, his elbow propping up his torso for a bit, as if he had been trying to turn over. When Manab, shocked speechless, pointed the beam at his face he saw BB frothing at the mouth, some of it having dribbled onto the floor.

Meanwhile, Pratap exclaimed loudly. "*Arre*[35]! Kunj Bihari is unconscious… frothing at his mouth!"

Manab, who was kneeling beside the prone form of BB, looked back and spotted Kunj Bihari lying flat on his back with foam bubbling at his mouth.

"Quick! Turn him on his side!" he said and turned back to examining BB. He shook him by his shoulder and called his name. No response. He was breathing though which was a positive sign. He shook him harder while speaking over his shoulder.

"BB is out too… and he's also frothing at the mouth… how…?"

He got up with a start. Where was Shambhu?

"Pratap, try to revive them while I look for Shambhunath!" He went out.

He called out loudly for Shambhu a couple of times but there was no response; nor had he expected that, to be honest. He swept the beam of light systematically from one side to the other, reaching the usual spot where he usually dozed and later, slept. No sign. He moved further out then a thought struck him and he turned back to the spot where Bihari cooked their meals.

Sure enough, he spotted Shambhu there right away, prone on the ground on his chest with the now expected foam around his mouth. It was clear he had staggered there to splash water when he had collapsed without having achieved that objective.

Manab squatted beside him and shone the light on his face. The

---

[35] An exclamation, a conversation filler

expression was identical to the others. The cold was severe, and that direct exposure wasn't doing any good. He tried lifting him but Shambhu was a deadweight, too heavy for Manab to carry. He called loudly for Pratap to help him.

Some fifteen minutes or so later, having lit the lamps, they cleaned up the three men to the best of their ability. Then they laid them in some comfort on the pair of mattresses there and covered them with a couple of bedsheets since they couldn't find the usual blankets. Pratap reported the cashbox had been cleaned out and was lying open with the key in its keyhole. Robbery was clearly the reason for the situation at hand.

Then, Manab called up Control.

"Singh-ji, situation is grim here. All three are unconscious and frothing at the mouth. We've cleaned them up some, but they need medical attention. Thankfully, they're breathing…And, the cashbox was opened, and all money stolen. Robbery is the reason."

Singh sounded quite concerned. "Robbery… I see! But why the frothing you think?"

"Poison… can't think what else would cause all three the same symptoms! Food poisoning is my guess…"

Pratap pointed at the utensils lying there; they were clean, with no remains of food they must have eaten for dinner. Could Bihari have collapsed after having cleaned up? Somehow, that didn't seem likely. Manab relayed that information too which added to the mystery of the situation.

"Singh-ji, I say we take them quickly to Mokameh and hospitalise them. Meanwhile, we can depute three temporary staff until the morning shift staff come in to take charge. Okay?"

"Yes, they'd be hospitalised quickly, I agree. Okay, take them all back to Mokameh. Who will you depute for the rest of the night there?"

"I'll think of something, not to worry. But let's move fast on this."

"Okay."

Immediately after this they moved the three unconscious men to the engine, much to the bewilderment of the drivers, and travelled back to Mokameh at normal speed for the line was secure since Manab set the Line Clear machine to "going on" from Rajendra Pul that Pankaj confirmed with his "coming on" setting.

It took them barely twenty minutes to reach Mokameh. Manab had called Pankaj ahead to have an ambulance standing by so transferring them to the hospital didn't take any additional time. Pratap accompanied them while Manab arranged for the replacement crew for Rajendra Pul. He asked Pankaj to get him two off-duty staff, a porter and a leverman. He himself stepped in as replacement for Bholenath.

Since the line was secure after their recent trip up and down, it was okay to despatch the much-delayed freight train. Once the replacement staff arrived, they hitched a ride on the same train to Rajendra Pul.

It wasn't until the next day evening that Manab found time to meet BB in the hospital. He had heard some sketchy details, but he wanted to hear it from BB himself.

He found him propped up on his bed, reading a book. BB had asked his family to not worry and not to unnecessarily come over to see him.

"BB!" Manab walked in, still in uniform. "How're you?"

A broad smile spread on his face. "Thanks to you, *dada*, and Pratap, I'm fine… we're all fine. No lingering effects!"

After the initial few minutes of greetings, thanks, and their swift waving away, Manab got to the point he was eager to discuss.

"So, BB, tell me in detail what happened the day before?"

BB narrated the whole story thereafter, Manab closely following and occasionally asking clarification questions.

"We sat down to dinner around 2200 hours or thereabouts… that lone passenger… Kesoram, joining but sitting a little distance away. When Bihari asked him to sit closer he declined saying he didn't want to disturb me. We let him be… but now I know why he chose to sit far!"

Manab smiled wryly. "I can imagine why… go on, BB."

He looked pensive for a bit. "Nothing more, really. About half an hour later… Bihari and Shambhu both had gone from there, Bihari to clean up and Shambhu for his post dinner *khaini* when I started feeling uneasy and in a very short while I started retching… I ran out and vomited, feeling very nauseated, then came inside to drink some water… I was sweating, even in that cold but even before I could reach the bottle on my desk, I fell…"

Manab could see him reliving those moments. He waited. BB continued after a minute.

"I felt I was dying then… my mouth felt icky… and I could feel froth in my mouth, gummy… and then I felt I was losing consciousness rapidly… my eyes were drooping, that infinite sleep was certain. I just managed to turn to a side… my last conscious act… so that I wouldn't choke on that awful froth… then what I know is waking up in this hospital!"

Manab was quiet for a minute. Then he asked, "I heard all of you were poisoned with *datura*[36]… so that passenger is the culprit, right?"

BB nodded. "Yes, that's what the doctor said… *Datura* poisoning… Bihari suspects Kesoram must have dumped the poison into the *sabzi* when he had gone to fetch a bucket of water… had you not

---

[36] Datura Stronium or Thornapple; The leaves and seeds specially are narcotic and have been used by bandits in India to drug victims causing deep sleep as they have narcotic and sedative effects

reached there when you did, things might have gotten far worse…" He looked up, his eyes moist.

"I've a small daughter, *dada*…" He sighed, then smiled. "But that was not to be!"

After a brief pause, Manab continued.

"You didn't see Bihari lying there? Or seen Shambhu around?"

"No… I's too ill to notice anything…"

"So… this, what's his name? Kesoram… clever fellow, he cleaned out the utensils to remove all trace of the poison. Anyway, so, he stole the cash…"

BB sighed. "There was a little more than 2,000 rupees cash in the cashbox… that is gone, *dada*, yes." He put his right hand up and wriggled his fingers to catch Manab's eyes.

"He also stole my gold rings, *dada*… see the marks?"

Manab could see the lighter skin where the rings had been.

"One of the them was my wedding ring, *dada*… belonged to my *sasur*[37]… my wife will be upset!"

Manab smiled. "On the contrary, Bhole Baba, she'll be glad that it went lightly… just your rings were stolen and you're safe!"

"Anything else lost?" he asked after a pause.

BB nodded. "Yes, I heard Bihari's silver chain is gone too… thankfully, Shambhu didn't have much cash… just 5-10 rupees… Bihari had no cash with him… Seems he also took our blankets!"

"Hmm." Manab sat in thought. "The police have taken your statement?"

"Yes, *dada*, Inspector Yadav was here. The Minapur *thana*[38] SHO[39]

---

[37] Father-in-law

[38] Police station

[39] Station House Officer, the officer in charge of a police station

was here too, *daroga*[40] Bhushan Singh. They're not hopeful… said it was likely this Kesoram fellow doesn't belong hereabouts and would have long escaped. Maybe he had some accomplices waiting nearby whom he'd joined and skipped… Imagine, *dada*. He ate our food… our salt! Accepted our hospitality and look what he did!" BB sounded sad.

"But that was his objective! To allay your suspicions and then rob you! Listen… The most important thing is, all three of you are safe and the doctor says you should be discharged tomorrow… this poison needs 24-36 hours to wear off and it is better to be in hospital till then. While 36 hours will be up soon, staying overnight is safer… that's the important thing!" Manab emphasised.

BB smiled. "You're right, *dada*. We'd focus on the positives!"

They smiled.

All three returned to their duties a couple of days later with no detrimental long-term effects on their health from the poisoning. However, the hopelessness of the police proved to be right. Kesoram was never found.

---

[40] Inspector

4

The Locked Waiting Room

The sky was barely light, stars still visible brightly. The coming dawn was still gathering momentum and the heat of the day was a few hours away. Only a few people had stirred yet, washing faces, cleaning teeth with a *datuan*[41] or just yawning, trying to chase away the last vestiges of sleep. Even Ghanshyam, the tea stall man, one of the first to get up in the mornings, was yet to get his wood fired stove going. Mokameh station was just thinking of setting the jack under its recumbent self.

A lady walked along the platform, clearly avoiding the splotches of light cast by the occasional overhead lamps. She was tall, impeccably attired in a dark chiffon sari, exquisitely proportioned, with her long, lustrous hair hanging down free to her waist. She had a stylish handbag slung over her right shoulder, her head bent down, avoiding any possible eye contact with the admittedly few people on the platform. Ahead of her strode Kailash, furtive and quick, with a small suitcase in hand.

One or two of the few there did cast her a look for she did appear out of place there, so well-groomed and that early in the morning but none took any further interest. The lady continued her sedate walk till she reached a pillar behind which she stopped, hidden from prying eyes. Kailash too stopped there. They were clearly expectant.

Just then a sleepy voice crackled over the announcement system. In its usual garbled diction, it announced the imminent arrival of the Gaya passenger train. That elicited only the barest reactions from

---

[41] A twig, usually of Neem, chewed on to clean teeth; traditional use

the assorted few that were present. When the train steamed in, some 15 minutes later, the somnolence was barely altered. A few detrained and only a handful boarded it including the lady in the chiffon sari. Kailash lugged the suitcase over and a few currency notes were pressed into his hands by the lady after which he left swiftly. The train tooted a couple of times and chugged out a few minutes later, bearing the mysterious lady away deeper into the gathering dawn.

Later the same day, sometime around 1100 hours, an argument was underway in the station master's office.

"The least I can say is the crates have not been received at this station!" Manab spoke into the phone receiver with exasperation creeping into his voice. For the last half an hour and more he had been leaving no stone unturned to locate half a dozen crates that had been despatched a few days ago from Bhopal. The intended recipient was fuming at his desk, his porters were flailing uselessly, and the crates remained elusive with startling determination.

The portly man across his desk wiped his forehead with a sodden handkerchief, steam misting his bifocals. He jabbed an indignant forefinger in the general direction of Manab and accused him of complete dereliction of duty.

"Station master, you have to find my boxes! My property was under your custody and there's no way you can lose them!"

Manab breathed deeply, trying to control his temper that was threatening to run away quickly. He slammed the phone down into its cradle and looked from under furrowed brows at Hariya.

"Hariya, have you looked in the store rooms at the end of the 4th platform? Sometimes they stow boxes there…"

Hariya wrung his hands and whined, "Yes, *sahib*, even that I have checked… no crates!"

Manab knew Hariya would have checked that but nevertheless one had to demonstrate thoroughness.

"Gupta-ji, your crates will be found. Your papers say they've been despatched and Indian Railways will never lose booked freight… perhaps they've been wrongly loaded on a different train. Give me a little time and I will track them down, you'll get them." He purposefully kept his voice toned down, infused with reasonableness.

The portly Gupta rolled his eyes as if the ridiculousness of the situation was beyond belief. He took his glasses off and wiped his oily, wet face with the rag in his hand. It was hard to be sure if that reduced or increased the wetness on his face.

"How can you load my boxes onto a different train altogether?" He made it sound as if Manab had personally pulled that impossible trick off.

"It's like this, Gupta-ji." Manab leaned back and gazed at the whirling fan in the ceiling, seeming to draw fortitude from it. "We load thousands of tonnes of freight every single day across hundreds of stations in the country… sometimes, very, very few times, a few boxes get wrongly loaded… but we locate them each and every time and ensure their safe delivery to the correct recipients… none is lost, trust me."

Gupta cocked an unbelieving eye at Manab. "All that's fine, Master *sahib*, but how many thousand tonnes of freight do you load at Bhopal station alone?"

The sly tone of that last repartee almost got Manab's goat completely. He wanted to vent his accumulated ire, really let fly and he would have, disregarding the consequences, when he was thankfully—in hindsight—interrupted by another harried man in damp clothes barging in, ahead of a flustered Nandu.

"What's this, Station Master? Why am I not allowed to rest in the first class waiting room?"

It was apparently a day for tough questions.

Gupta turned to look at the newcomer with a bemused expression: "Indian Railways at their best!" it seemed to mock. Manab cast a belligerent eye at Nandu then turned towards the irate gentleman.

"Please sit down, sir." He courteously pointed at another vacant chair across his desk. "Hariya, get the gentleman some cold water from the pitcher!"

Nandu had stepped up to pull the chair out and solicitously seated him. This courteousness helped bring the temper down a notch evidently as the man drank the water greedily. Manab waited patiently while Gupta bided his time, someone else's distress helping perhaps to mitigate some of his own.

Once the man had put down the glass on the table, Manab asked him politely. "Yes, sir, what seems to be the problem? How can I help you?"

Some of the old irritability resurfaced on the sweaty face of the man. "Why can't your staff open the waiting room for me? Why is it locked in the first place?"

Keeping his tone polite but firm, Manab spoke, "Sir, may I see your ticket?"

The man seemed to swell a bit. "You think I'm not eligible to enter the first class waiting room?" He pulled the little piece of stiff card from his shirt pocket, slightly marked with sweat, and thrust it into Manab's hand who inspected it briefly, noting the validity and the class. The indignant man was well within his rights to demand to wait in the first class waiting room, after all.

Only now Manab focussed attention on Nandu. "Why is the waiting room not being opened for…" he paused to squint at the scrawl on the ticket still in his hand. "For ah, Mr. Tiwari?"

"*Sahib*…" There was a strong sense of hesitation in Nandu's reply. Finally, he blurted out, "*Sahib*, I cannot find Kailash!"

"Eh?"

"Yes *sahib*, he was the one who had the early morning shift… he mustn't have put the keys back in the proper place."

Manab tapped his fingers on the desk, irritation seeping through them. "You've looked thoroughly for him?" When Nandu nodded vigorously he went on, "All the platforms? The other waiting rooms? His other usual haunts?"

While Nandu nodded right through the list of possible locations, Hariya motioned discreetly and spoke, "*Sahib*, he has a place I know… give me a few minutes, I'll find the keys!" And with that he was off.

A cackling laugh startled Manab out of his bemused wonder. Gupta's sarcasm was unmistakable. Manab forced himself to concentrate on Tiwari instead.

"Just wait here sir for a few minutes. He'll soon be back with the keys…"

The man snorted. "I hope he's quick! My family is waiting outside the waiting room… in this heat!"

Gupta picked up his theme again. "So, Master-*sahib*, what about my boxes?"

"Gupta-ji, not to worry. I will personally call you when I've located them. I'll have them delivered here without fail!"

Gupta, not quite convinced, left soon after while the first-class passenger fumed, his patience wearing thin by the minute. Thankfully Hariya returned a few minutes later, beaming across his pock-marked face, keys held aloft triumphantly.

Manab wanted Tiwari out of his room as quickly as possible and didn't pause to ask him where Hariya had found Kailash. "There you go Mr. Tiwari! My apologies but now you can go to the waiting room and wait for your train. Nandu, go with Mr. Tiwari and ready the room for him and his family!"

And thus ended the morning's fracas.

A few days later, in the stiflingly hot afternoon, as Manab was catching up with his paperwork, Hariya sidled in and stood to one side, quietly hopping from one foot to the other. Manab hadn't initially noticed him but the frequent movement caught his eye finally.

"Yes, Hariya, what is it?"

At times Hariya would adopt an attack-the-core-and-answer-background-questions-when-asked strategy to relate some incident, which admittedly tested Manab's patience. This was one of those times.

"Same thing happened *sahib*!"

Manab looked blankly at the porter. Nothing clicked in his mind.

"*Sahib*! Kailash! Again he was not to be found… and a first-class passenger demanding the waiting room be opened for him!"

Manab made a valiant attempt to keep his temper from flaring but promised himself he would deal with the errant porter at the earliest. Such flagrant irresponsibility just could not be allowed. For now, he merely wriggled his brows at Hariya. "Speak up!" they commanded.

"*Sahib*, I went looking for him in his hidey-hole… that unused three tier coach parked beyond platform 3. You remember *sahib*? He goes there to nap!"

"And?" Manab kept his annoyance in check.

A little crestfallen at this apparent lack of indignation, Hariya continued, "And I got the waiting room keys from him… its settled now," he ended somewhat sheepishly.

"Good work, Hariya. I'll have a word with Kailash later." And gesturing at Hariya to leave he went back to his files though reminding himself to speak to Kailash without fail later that evening.

It was only after a few days that Manab remembered his promise to himself. One evening, as Manab stopped by Ghanshyam's tea stall for a quick cuppa and a general catch-up on the latest gossip, his fickle memory decided to kick in unannounced upon seeing Kailash passing by.

"Kailash!"

"*Sahib*?" The man in question halted and waited respectfully.

"What is this about you not keeping the first class waiting room keys in the proper place? And going off to sleep during duty hours?" Manab decided to be direct.

A furtive look came over Kailash's face. Clearly the man had something to hide.

"*Sahib…*" he faltered. But Manab's stern look prompted him to continue. A few gulps interrupted his narration, which was, as it turned out, a confession.

What emerged eventually could be condensed to a few broad facts: Kailash had the responsibility to clean up the first class waiting room besides his other morning duties. Post which he felt the need for a nap and for which, unknown to everyone, he made for the abandoned coach at the bottom of platform 3 and took a refreshing siesta.

The point of why he didn't park the key at the expected spot irked Manab, so he pressed for an answer. That was, Kailash explained, because he wanted keenly to avoid anyone who could potentially prevent his escape to his secret spot.

Something about his story didn't ring true to Manab. He couldn't quite put his finger on it, but something was off… then decided he wouldn't press for it just then.

"Hmm… I see." He cocked a sceptical eye at Kailash. "You know that is dereliction of duty and I could charge you with it, right?"

Kailash gulped frantically, real fright in his eyes. He could lose his job. "*Sahib!*"

Manab looked grim but before he could say anything further, Kailash tumbled on, incoherent in his anxiety and hurry. "I'll never repeat them, *sahib*! No more napping… promise, I promise you!" and so on in similar vein until Manab relented.

"Okay, Kailash, be warned then! One more complaint and you'll be out, understood?"

The next Thursday, the Gaya passenger was delayed by several hours due to some problems with the tracks and a sequence of events was triggered that had great impact on the peace of Manab's mind. The first inkling was again an irate first-class passenger.

The announcement on the PA system had just been made regarding the delay in the arrival of the Gaya passenger when Nandu burst into Manab's office with a self-important looking man striding in after him.

"*Sahib*! Kailash is not to be found again and this gentleman is unable to use the first class waiting room as the door is locked!"

Swearing to himself he would soon settle Kailash's hash after this recurrence, Manab ordered, "Get Hariya, ask him to find Kailash in the abandoned coach!"

He got the fuming man seated, assuring him of immediate resolution and stepped out of his office, intending to get into the matter himself.

As he strode off towards the waiting room, he saw Nandu haring back.

"*Sahib*, Hariya and I both found Kailash together… right at the waiting room! There's a lady with him!"

"Eh?" Manab had no clue but he snapped out his decision. "Take the man waiting in my office immediately to the waiting room and settle that matter. And ask Kailash to come to my office along with that lady. Go now!"

He waited impatiently for the duo to make an appearance and about ten minutes later Kailash entered the office hesitantly carrying a small suitcase followed by the woman.

Manab caught his breath involuntarily. The woman was completely unlike any other that he had ever seen. Her presence radiated authority, her grooming impeccable and poise impossible to tackle. Attired in a pale blue chiffon sari, hair loose and pulled over her left shoulder, she struck a magnificent figure. She was very fair, her features regular, with a hint of amusement in her lustrous eyes. Definitely not young but it was impossible to bracket her into any specific age group. She could be in her late twenties or mid-forties… there was no way to be certain.

Manab felt powerless. His mind was without mooring and he couldn't think of a thing to say. And to make it worse, the woman seemed to guess that effortlessly. She laughed softly—in someone less dignified one could say she giggled but, in this case, definitely not. It was painfully clear to Manab that she knew she had this effect on people, especially younger men.

Manab turned his gaze towards Kailash, a woolly thought burgeoning there that he could perhaps pin that man down with better effect. But the woman pre-empted that completely.

In a low-pitched voice that perfectly complemented her appearance, she said, "Permit me, Mr. Banerjee. Poor Kailash has nothing to do with this."

With unmatched grace, she walked up to Manab's desk, slung her handbag on the back of a wooden chair, and seated herself, gesturing quite patronizingly for Manab to also take his seat.

Manab obeyed without demur, as if it was the most natural thing to do. Kailash gawked, silent. That she even knew his name quite completed his mystification. Who was this woman?

As if she'd read his innermost thought, she spoke. "My name is Maya Devi, Mr. Banerjee. I pass by your station quite frequently. And, a rather neatly maintained station, I must say." Her smile lit his office up.

This compliment only served to accentuate Manab's state of confusion. "I-I don't understand, Maya-ji…"

Switching tacks, she continued. "Please don't blame poor Kailash for anything, Mr. Banerjee. He has only been following my instructions."

"I-instructions?"

"Yes… you see, I need the waiting room to rest until my train comes. There're a few hours between my trains. I've therefore instructed Kailash to keep the waiting room available and then lock it discreetly after I leave. That's all."

As if that explained everything.

Manab's expression must have been loud and clear for Maya Devi took up her explanation again, a touch more patiently this time.

"I take the Gaya passenger, Mr. Banerjee. That normally departs here at 0520 hours. And I reach the station around 0130 hours. Those few hours I use your waiting room. The train was much delayed today and thus this…" she pointed at herself expressively, "interview…" Her smile was warm with not a hint of embarrassment.

While the mists of confusion swirled still in Manab's mind, he at least understood the basics of the story now.

"I see…" he slowly said. "And you recruited Kailash to enable this little arrangement…"

Her laughter tinkled. "Yes! After all he had to stay awake, unlock the room… keep it clean, carry my suitcase. A just compensation was called for you'll agree surely?"

At no time did she indicate she had been doing anything wrong. Manab resolved in his mind he would put an end to this arrangement. Just as he was about to act on this, the Gaya passenger steamed in, accompanied by an announcement to that effect. Maya Devi stood up, grace personified.

"I must go now, Mr. Banerjee. It was nice talking to you." She smiled and swung her handbag to her shoulder.

"Kailash!" She commanded. The man scurried to pick up her suitcase. She had almost reached the door when she turned back.

"Oh, Mr. Banerjee!" She retraced her steps to his desk behind which he stood still. Before his stunned eyes, she dipped into her handbag and took out a handful of cash, about half an inch thick.

"Please, take this! Don't say no! Just a little something…"

At last Manab reacted. "No!" Sharper than he had perhaps intended. "No! I cannot take that!"

"Of course, you must! Think of it as a gift from your elder sister… now, come on!"

And into his unwilling but nerveless hands she thrust the wad of currency and walked swiftly out, Kailash in bemused tow.

For how long Manab stood there with money in his fist he didn't know. Snapping out of it suddenly, his eyes dropped to the money in his hands and dropped that on his desk in shock.

So much money! He quickly counted the notes: 2,100 rupees! His hands shook. What did the lady do to be able to casually give away so much money? The unavoidable truth was rather frightening. Something illegal…! He forced himself to calm down. Surely it was also possible she was very rich and could afford to throw money away? As he debated with himself, the one thing that stood out was that he would *never* use that money. But the biggest mystery remained: who was Maya Devi?

He put the money in an envelope, sealed it and then carefully locked that in his drawer, resolving to solve the mystery. Then, as happens often enough, daily life interfered and this matter slipped from his mind until one day the sight of Kailash going about his duties brought the memories out in a rush.

He called Kailash over and asked, "Kailash? Has that lady visited again?"

A guilty look passed over his face. "No *sahib*… not since that day when she met you."

"Hmm." Manab scratched his chin. "Who is she?"

Kailash's reaction was quick and tinged with fear. "Don't know *sahib*, honest! She gave me money and I thought the waiting room was anyway unused in the night… so no harm in letting her use it…" He smiled ingratiatingly, nervousness flecked around his face. "And *sahib*, a few paise in addition to help my poor family… no harm to anyone… no one knows also…" he rambled on.

Manab waved him off wearily. He decided he would find the answer from old Jha of the Wheeler book store the same evening.

Jha-ji proved to be as good a source of information as always. That evening Manab made it a point to remember to look him up at the bookshop. As he reached there, eager to ask his questions, he found Jha stepping from behind the counter to go for his evening tea.

"Arre Banerjee-*babu*? Aren't you coming for tea now? Come, come!" He started walking away forcing Manab to follow.

After Ghanshyam served them, Manab held Jha's elbow and pulled him aside a bit. "Jha-ji, I need some information."

Taking a leisurely sip, Jha made some encouraging sounds.

"Jha-ji, you know about that woman who rests in the first class waiting room occasionally? Early morning? Kailash has been helping her…?"

A curious look entered Jha's eyes. About to sip his tea, he paused, holding that for a few beats. Manab knew things seldom escaped Jha's attention. He wondered why Jha was sizing up his response for he clearly was.

"Ye…es, I do know… why do you ask? You've already met her… you know who she is, surely?"

Manab looked deep into Jha's eyes, trying to figure out the reason for his evasiveness.

"All I know, Jha-ji, is her name… Maya Devi. And I don't know if that is even her real name!"

Jha laughed softly to himself. He finished his tea in a long gulp and said, "Oh yes, that is indeed her name… Maya Devi." Then his face grew serious. He dropped his voice a few notches and spoke, dead serious.

"Master-*sahib*, this is very serious. She is… how do I say… not very good news."

Manab gaped at Jha; what was the man saying? Dangerous?

"What do you mean!" It wasn't a question any longer.

In answer, Jha looked keenly from under his wrinkled brows. "Tell me, have you heard of Bachha Singh, Banerjee-*babu*?"

It took Manab several seconds to tackle that seemingly tangential question. "Bachha Singh? You mean that Bachha Singh, the notorious gold smuggler Bachha Singh?"

"The very same, Banerjee-*babu*, the very same."

Manab's blood ran cold. What the connection was between that mysterious lady and the dreaded criminal was yet unknown. Bachha Singh was reputed to have murdered several people and ran a smuggling empire that had tentacles in distant lands, or so it was rumoured. People whispered that he literally owned a few politicians too and thus roamed around in freedom, indeed surrounded by his gang of armed men; none dared to question or hinder him.

The next obvious question followed. Manab asked, "So what does Maya Devi do?"

Jha took a minute or two before replying. "No one can say for sure, Banerjee-*babu*… perhaps she is a courier? Perhaps she carries bundles of gold in her suitcase? Who can say? Indeed, who will question her?"

Manab imagined that magnificently poised lady, impeccably attired… and it defied him to connect her with the image of a common smuggler.

Meanwhile, Jha continued. "All I know is that she visits Nepal every month… and she stops by here on her return journey, changing trains."

Suddenly the vision of a bundle of crackling currency notes sprang painfully in Manab's mind.

"Jha-ji!" He exclaimed loudly then lowered his voice as Jha looked quizzically at him. "She left a large sum of money with me, Jha-ji She said I was to take it as a gift from an elder sister!"

Jha again kept quiet for a couple of minutes, eyes slowly crinkling in a smile, while Manab fretted.

"Banerjee-*babu*, that's a good sign then… you must have impressed her in some manner. My advice is keep that money and forget about the entire incident. Good for everyone! Don't you think?"

"No!" Manab was too scared. "No, not at all, Jha-ji! How can I keep that money? That's criminal money!"

"And what do you intend to do then?"

"I-I will return the money… next time when she is here, I will return it!"

Jha laid a kindly hand on his shoulder. "Think it over, Banerjee-*babu*. You're a young man, impetuous… perhaps some deliberation will help you straighten your thoughts, huh? Why do something that is best avoided?"

Manab felt he would gain nothing in trying to convince Jha of his need to return that money but it was clear as daylight to him that he simply had to return it, somehow, anyhow. The thought that accepting that money would somehow imply his soul was owned by Bachha Singh's cohorts was unbearable.

He nodded. "Hmm… perhaps you're right! Yes, I'll think it over, Jha-ji…" He looked at his friend. "But thank you for helping me see the full picture, Jha-ji. At least some of the mystery is solved!"

The clatter of changing tracks for the speeding train awakened Manab from his nap. The breeze was cool in his face as the train rushed towards Calcutta where he had some work over the following couple of days. He had had his dinner and was reading a novel by the window when he had slipped into the nap. It had been his usual long, tiring day… he shook his head with a wry smile and checked the time: well past 2200 hours. The night outside was a passing melange of silhouettes, dark and mysterious. His one co-passenger in the first-class cabin he shared with had turned in, sound asleep in his bunk, gentle snores underlining that. He decided it was time for him to also get some sleep. Decision made, he went down the corridor to the toilet.

Two months had passed since that chat with Jha and the mysterious lady had yet to make a reappearance. Manab had waited impatiently, fretting and anxious, for her to appear but she had not. He tasked Kailash with informing him, day, or night, immediately of her arrival but that just didn't happen. The money remained as he had first packed it in an envelope, untouched. But it managed to irk him long distance.

As he was returning to his cabin he noticed a woman swiftly entering a cabin down the corridor. He stood stock still. Something about that woman struck him forcefully, the way she had carried herself, something he couldn't quite put his finger on… but she seemed more than familiar. As this went through his mind in seconds, his cognitive skills finally kicked in: it was that mysterious Maya Devi! Talk about coincidences!

Manab rushed down the corridor without further thought, no plan in mind to deal with the confrontation. The only thought that gripped him completely was his need to return the money. It mattered little that he wasn't carrying that envelope; he had enough cash with him to return that amount then and there.

He paused at the door. She had shut it—naturally—and he hesitated there, prudence finally getting a chance to insinuate herself. But that reluctance was momentary, he knocked on the door; he'd always apologise and beat a hasty retreat if he turned out to be wrong.

The door slid open a fraction and an eye, large and fearless, could be seen.

"Yes?" The voice was stern but didn't seem to belie any tension at this unexpected invasion of privacy.

"Er… madam…" Manab felt inexplicably tongue-tied, the common malady of a decent person reluctant to commit a *faux pas*. But he needn't have worried. The next thing took him by surprise.

The door slid open all the way, and a smiling Maya Devi stood in front, still impeccably attired in sari.

"Mr. Banerjee, come in." And she stood aside to let a bewildered Manab enter the cabin. He subconsciously noted it was a coupé with no second occupant.

"You… remember me?"

She laughed gently. "Of course, I do, station master *sahib*. It's not often I meet honest officials…"

As Manab looked wonderingly at this strange woman, she continued, "Nothing to wonder about, Banerjee-*babu*, I get information…" She didn't elaborate further.

Manab's curiosity surged. Information? Did she mean one of his staff passed it on to her? Who? Kailash?

The initiative still lay with her. "So, tell me, Banerjee-*babu*, how can I help you?"

They had sat down on the bunk in the meanwhile, and Manab struggled to bring the topic up. He summoned his courage.

"Maya-ji, it's about that money. Remember?"

She didn't nod or give any outward signal of acknowledging that but neither did she deny, she just kept quiet.

Manab decided to plunge ahead. "I must return that money to you, Maya-ji. I cannot accept it."

There, he had done it. Or at least, had said it. Again.

"And I'd told you to accept it as a gift from an elder sister, Banerjee-*babu*." Her mouth curled gently into a smile.

"I-I cannot… that money…" his voice trailed off. He just couldn't bring himself to say the money was tainted with crime.

She was quiet for a long moment. "There's no danger to you, Banerjee-*babu*. I've made sure of that…"

"Eh? Danger…?"

"Perhaps that is what is preying on your mind?" She paused, smiled, and then said, "Perhaps you've heard… some tales? Yes?"

That was undeniable. He didn't say anything, but the astute lady gathered what she needed for her confirmation of her theory. She smiled, no malice in it.

"You're a good man, Banerjee-*babu*. And courageous… to grab hold of an opportunity for which you surely hadn't planned… yes, courageous."

Manab could say nothing. Some subliminal message told him she would accept the money. He took his wallet out, extracted a sheaf of currency notes, quickly counted out 2,100 rupees, folded the bundle and held it out to her. And she took the money, putting it casually under her handbag that lay on the bunk between them.

"No harm will ever come to you, Banerjee-*babu*, in these areas where you're posted. Take it from an elder sister." Her voice was quiet, her face serious.

"Thank you, Maya-ji." Manab didn't know what else to say. He rose slowly to leave.

Maya Devi spoke again, her voice back to her usual light tone, a smile tugging at her mouth. "You're a young man, Banerjee-*babu*… you should be getting married soon. Let me know if you need some exquisite *zari*[42] for your new wife…"

As Manab left, a smile emerging on his face with the burden finally off his back, Maya Devi smiled back, ingenuous, and warm.

---

[42] Silver or gold thread-work in garments, including saris

5

Murda Jaga![43]

Ramsaran hurried through platform number 6 of the Patna Junction station, eyes peeled for Mukund Bihari, the guard scheduled for the Patna-Gaya passenger that stood steaming at the same platform. It was 2255 hours, just a few minutes away from departure of that train and Mukund Bihari was nowhere to be found. Around him, last minute passengers hurried to board, while a few were filling water bottles at the fountains, some buying fruits—whoever ate them in the middle of the night anyway—and some others, biscuits, or other snacks, to presumably keep body and soul together. At that late hour, only a handful of shops were open, mostly those that were around the train.

About half an hour earlier, the night shift ASM, Manab Banerjee, had called Ramsaran to urgently find Mukund. He should have reported earlier but had not. As the scheduled guard on the Patna-Gaya passenger train, set to depart at 2300 hours, he had to take charge. Going missing this close to a scheduled departure was naturally a cause for concern.

Only it was not really uncommon for Mukund to disappear occasionally. He was a middle-aged man who really loved his liquor, and found every opportunity to indulge it. He had been reprimanded many times and even come close to being charge-sheeted but had managed to avoid causing any scheduling mishap and thus, escaped official censure. The habit had also made him a butt of numerous jokes, some quite gruesome, and somewhat paradoxically, a sought-

---

[43] Literally, "Dead man come alive!"

after companion as well by those that had the glad-eyes for the amber liquid, for Mukund was known to be quite generous to his drinking buddies.

Ramsaran reached the end of platform 6 with nary a trace of the missing guard. As he scratched his head and wondered where to look next, Manab fretted impatiently outside his office on platform 1, constantly looking at his wristwatch, willing it to run slow. In desperation, he had asked for a replacement guard to be deployed but such a step would make a delayed departure a certainty. And that would not be welcome. For the replacement guard to be informed—a porter had already started for his home—then for him to get ready, reach the station, take charge and signal departure, close to an hour would be lost. Appalling!

This close to departure with no solution to make that departure time, the announcement had to be made to that effect. He instructed the appropriate announcement to be made therefore, and listened with only half an ear to the subsequent garbled message on the PA system. He grumbled under his breath; Mukund had finally slipped up but it had to happen on his watch!

The summer night in Patna was oppressive, which was of course par for the course at this time of the year. The monsoon was many weeks away; the heat tended to be scorching and sunset was no guarantee for pleasant evenings. People considered themselves lucky if a storm would briefly blow to cool things down a bit.

Manab was on the night shift, which, like in his initial years, he didn't mind handling since it gave him relatively a little more peace. A couple of years ago, the year India had won the first one day international championship, the Prudential World Cup in England, he had finally been transferred to Patna Junction. Initially he had been on cabin duties but after a year of doing that he had been made in-charge of platforms. This entailed more public dealings as all passenger issues were his responsibility, as were protocol duties, cleanliness, health, and so on.

Personally, he was in the pink of his marriage bliss. Pretty as a picture, Mita had come into Manab's life some six years ago, about half a year after he had the minor adventure with Maya Devi, the *zari* smuggler. It was an arranged marriage of course and he had been wary, but things had turned out really well. And about a year ago, their daughter Keya was born, cute as a button and fatherhood was, he was discovering every day, a voyage of learning, wonderment, and worry. Married life rather agreed with him.

As it always happened when a delay was announced, he had to deal with some irate passengers. He apologized and told them the truth, emphasizing the need for safety if a guard was missing. He had found that people tended to cool down significantly if he dealt with them openly and honestly, and if no regulations were broken or safety was compromised, when he told them the truth behind such delays. He took pride in seldom letting issues escalate to the Station Manager, his senior at the station.

As he was speaking to one such upset self-important man, Ramnivas, the replacement guard for Mukund Bihari, reported for duty. Manab took a break from placating the gentleman and signed Ramnivas in for the guard's duty and sent him racing to take charge. It was 2350 hours; as he had expected, it had delayed the departure by almost an hour. Inwardly sighing, he turned back to the fuming man.

"Sir, the train will depart in the next few minutes now that we have the guard in place," he said, smiling conciliatingly.

A lot of the man's indignation had dissipated seeing the guard in place and with the realization that the ASM had been telling him the truth. He mumbled an incoherent 'okay' under his breath but shot a look at Manab that seemed to say that while he was mollified somewhat, all was not quite forgiven. As the man went off, Manab smiled wryly and turned back for his office. Behind him an announcement could be heard proclaiming the immediate departure of the Patna-Gaya passenger from platform 6.

Around 0100 hours, when Manab was taking a break outside on the platform, he spotted Ramsaran snoozing behind one of the pillars. That reminded him of the missing Mukund.

He tapped Ramsaran on his shoulder. "Ramsaran! Wake up…"

The dozing man jumped a bit and stood up quickly, rubbing his eyes. "I'm awake, *sahib*, totally awake!" The lie was too blatant to not laugh aloud at, which Manab did.

"Alright, alright, Ramsaran, no harm done. Tell me, did you find Mukund finally?"

"Mukund, *sahib*?" His eyes goggled for a bit. "No, *sahib*, nowhere!" He waved his arms around, sweeping the station in every direction. "I looked everywhere… couldn't find him anywhere…"

Manab rubbed his chin, a look of amused wonder creasing his brows, looking unseeingly across the platforms. "Uh huh… nowhere, huh…" He didn't see Ramsaran nodding vigorously in affirmation.

"Do you think he could have gone home?" He flicked a look at Ramsaran who shook his head as vigorously.

Mukund had been sighted in the station sometime before 2100 hours; this even Ravindra Sekhar, the new ASM who he had relieved from the start of his shift at 2200 hours, had confirmed.

Ramsaran didn't think he would have gone home where he would be facing the wrath of a much-harried wife. Was he then in some drunken stupor somewhere? An inexplicable stab of worry ran through Manab.

"Ramsaran, get a couple of porters and let's look for him thoroughly, shall we?"

When the head porter returned with two more of his men, Manab instructed them to look into every nook and cranny of the station for Mukund. Being a large station, there were hundreds of nice little cubby holes he could have had his little party in and then fallen, sozzled out of his mind.

"And remember, if you find him, don't awaken him right away! Call me first, okay?" was Manab's parting instruction.

They split into two parties and started their hunt, Manab and one burly guy named Kallu while Ramsaran paired up with the other man, who was universally called Pahelwan[44], a name that his physique lived up to comfortably.

There were a few rather convenient spots around the station that one could hope to burrow away in to avoid notice. The back of a store room, the roof of a cabin, inside any of the few abandoned coaches or a secluded corner behind the remotest building… they were all popular with those in need. Naturally, they formed the priority set of places to be searched. And Manab picked the coaches as his personal target. Armed with a torchlight, he went through them, initially with enthusiasm and then with waning energy until the last of them proved to be innocent of Mukund in any state. Then rousing himself up, he pushed for the other popular spots for hiding. They went from one to the next, but Mukund stayed firmly missing. Finally, Manab called his search party together on platform 1 for a brief confab.

"Ramsaran, Kallu and Pahelwan, this looks a little more serious now… we've spent, what, more than an hour looking for Mukund? And no sign of his hair or hide!"

The others stood, stoically silent. He instructed them to pair up again; Kallu and he would do the platforms 1 through 3 while the other two would do the rest.

As they moved out again, Manab reemphasized, "Remember! Check everywhere and if you find anyone lying somewhere wrapped in a sheet, pull that off to check! Okay?"

Platform 1 being the one that housed most of the administrative staff and offices, was, while being more crowded, the least preferred

---

[44] Wrestler; someone with a muscular physique

among those that wanted to shirk; there were just too many prying eyes to successfully stay hidden for long. Consequently, Kallu and he went through that fairly rapidly till the very edge of it, the point where it angled sharply down as a ramp that was used to move freight on carts. To one side at the end of the ramp someone lay covered in a tattered sheet, unusual for such summer nights. Manab gestured at Kallu to quickly check. The burly man bent and gingerly pulled the corner of that sheet when suddenly the man underneath sat up, round-eyed with fright.

"Oh…" Manab waved at Kallu to let the guy be; it was the thin, dark beggar with an unkempt, bushy beard, who lived around the station, scrounging a living somehow. No one quite knew his name for the man either couldn't speak or wouldn't. The beggar continued to stare at them with frightened eyes as both walked away.

As they worked their way down the broad length that housed platforms 2 and 3 on its either sides, Manab wondered where Mukund could have disappeared. He was aware of his tumultuous married life, the tumult mostly the outcome of his drunken bouts. He would occasionally disappear for up to a day—though never till tonight had he missed a scheduled duty—only to reappear, bedraggled and reeking of interesting smells, insincerely apologetic for a very short time. His clothes would proclaim where he had spent the night—that is when he pulled an all-nighter—muddy and dirty to announce a night spent in the comforts of a cosy ditch or with straws sticking in his hair to assert his repose in some handy *tabela*[45].

Other than his drunken escapades, Mukund Bihari was a quiet sort, never one to draw attention to himself. So, what could have happened? Had he finally snapped, run away from it all? Manab didn't quite believe that.

They had reached midway by then, the sight no different from what was standard for that time of the night, emptiness mostly, a few of

---

[45] Cowshed

the concrete seats occupied by sleeping people. These were usually a few *coolies* and an occasional passenger waiting for a train that they would board in the middle of the night or in the wee hours of the morning. As Manab stood and brooded, he was suddenly reminded of the famous old story by Edgar Allan Poe, *The Purloined Letter*. The core idea from that story had never left him: If you wished to hide something, hide it in plain sight!

"Kallu!" The man turned to look at him with unease. What was *sahib* going to propose now?

"Kallu! Check every sleeping man on the resting benches! Don't care if he is covered head to toe! Just pull that out and check! Quick, now, go!" And he hurried himself to the closest such bench with a sleeper.

Just the third bench proved to be lucky. And it was Manab himself who found the prone body with the head completely wrapped in a *gamchha*. He lay on his right with his face towards the backrest, legs bent at the knees and arms tucked in tightly. He was dressed in a pair of drab grey trousers and a shirt that appeared indeterminate in colour. Manab didn't hesitate. He shook him sharply by his shoulder.

There was no response. The man continued to sleep unperturbed. The light wasn't too bright there and the shape of the body as it lay there made it nearly impossible to be sure if it was Mukund. By then Kallu had come up also and at Manab's gesture, he pulled at the *gamchha,* but it was stuck tight under the head. With a cluck of irritation, Manab stepped forward and pulled it hard, causing the man's head to flip over to the left, facing straight up with the *gamchha* fully off his face. It was Mukund Bihari, completely oblivious to the world around him.

Manab shone his torchlight directly on his face. His eyes were shut and did not flinch at the sudden bright light. Manab shook him hard by his shoulder but again without any result. Then between Kallu and himself, they turned the sleeping man onto his back. This caused his left arm to slide off his belly and flop to the side, lifelessly. They could see his stomach rise and fall as he breathed; he was definitely alive. Curious, Manab leaned forward and delicately sniffed near his mouth and almost gagged. The stench of alcohol was overpowering.

Over the next few minutes, they tried everything they could think of to rouse the man but completely to no avail. Manab had spotted Ramsaran and Pahelwan on platform 4 and hailed them over. Each of them tried something but Mukund could not be awakened. Directly yelling near his ears or tickling his ribs or foot and making the man smell someone's soles yielded no results. Mukund stayed adamantly asleep.

Manab looked at his watch: it was well after 0230 hours; they must have been at it for the last fifteen minutes or more. He felt frustrated. Here was the missing man, finally found, but determinedly unresponsive, so drunk he was apparently. As he watched the others trying vainly to rouse the man, a wicked idea crossed Manab's mind and he chuckled to himself.

'You guys, stop!" He called out. The others turned to him and gaped. Manab continued, "Pick him and carry him over to platform 1, will you now? I'll tell you what next there. Now, pick him up!"

When Kallu tried to help Pahelwan, the latter waved his hand dismissively at him and picked him up easily in a fireman's lift. The drastic change in position or the fact that he was now being transported over another man's shoulder had no impact on his dead-to-the-world sleep. Mukund might have grunted once or twice but Manab couldn't be sure for they were moving swiftly.

On platform 1, none appeared awake. Manab indicated an empty bench for Pahelwan to park his burden, which he did quite unceremoniously, dumping Mukund hard on it. The sleeping man wasted no time in sliding out into a comfortable stretch and letting out a satisfied snore. The three porters stood with quizzical expressions on their faces, possibly wondering what Manab-*sahib* would have them do next.

"Now, Ramsaran, find a nice white bedsheet and get it here, will you?" Manab had a wolfish smile on his face.

When Ramsaran hesitated, Manab spoke almost brusquely. "*Arre*, go to the store and get one from there… tell the chap there that I have asked for one, okay?"

The fellow ran off on the errand and Manab rubbed his hands in glee. The other two maintained a deferential silence. Ramsaran was back in a few minutes with a crisp, clean folded bedsheet in his arms.

Manab took the next few minutes to give detailed instructions to the trio and got them to repeat them to ensure their clarity as well as to satisfy himself.

"Now go, you three! Once you've done what I have instructed you to do, Ramsaran, you come back and report to me. Understood?"

Ramsaran promised to return and give a detailed report. They left chuckling, once more with Pahelwan carrying the sleeping Mukund over his shoulder. Manab stood with a big smile plastered on his face and then made his way to his office.

The head porter led the others outside the station to the area beyond the portico, near the entrance by the road. It was dark despite the lampposts which cast splotches of light around. All shops in the vicinity were closed and a few vehicles were parked in the station's parking lot. There were the usual few people sleeping at random points around as well.

At the entrance were several low concrete platforms that served to segregate incoming traffic into different lanes for rickshaws, autorickshaws, cars, and buses. The trio reached the outermost such platform, Mukund still blissfully out of commission. Pahelwan carefully lowered him on the platform on his back, straightened his arms down the sides, and brought the feet together. Then Ramsaran and Kallu held the sheet open and placed it carefully on top of the recumbent form, tucking the edges and corners of the sheet underneath Mukund, until the entire body was covered in the white shroud, head to toe. Ramsaran then found a couple of half-bricks and placed one each above the man's head and below his feet, making the sheet quite unflappable. Meanwhile, Kallu had gone off to fetch a handful of discarded flowers from the *Bajrangbali*[46] temple that stood to one side beyond the station. They placed the flowers around Mukund's covered head, and on his chest. Then they stood back and surveyed their handiwork, grinning happily.

It looked exactly like a dead body laid out before its final journey. Ramsaran looked around and saw no one. They had done their deed precisely as they would have hoped to have accomplished. They headed back, with many a glance back at that admittedly macabre sight.

Ramasaran then went to Manab's office to report.

Manab looked up from his papers with a smile.

"Done, Ramsaran?"

The man chortled. "Yes, *sahib*, it is done! You'd see that… looks exactly like a dead body!"

"Hmm… and did you remember to put the few coins I gave on Mukund?"

A stricken look came over Ramsaran's face.

"No, *sahib*! I forgot! I'll run out and do that right away!"

He was back again in a few minutes, looking a little chastened.

"Done, *sahib*, I have dropped the coins randomly on and around the body."

"Okay. Now tell Kallu to keep an eye out on Mukund and ensure no one steals those coins…" Manab instructed and dismissed Ramsaran.

Mukund slept the sleep of the deeply contented. Or, more accurately, the sleep of the entirely sozzled. He didn't toss or turn. He didn't

---

[46] Lord Hanuman

care if the surface on which he lay was hard and anyway, the bench he had craftily selected out in the open on platform 3 had been equally hard. There was a light breeze that probably kept him cool. The night wore on, the stars moving across the heavens and as the hours seeped away, the eastern sky started to lighten. People were out and about now. There were a few passengers arriving to catch early morning trains. And a few trains also stopped from which alighted travellers come to Patna. The hubbub was building up.

As the people passed, the white-shrouded body attracted attention. Most did a quick, cursory one-handed forehead-and-chest taps in acknowledgement and uttered a brief prayer under the breath, but a few went up and dropped a few coins on or around what they believed was a dead body. As the dawn broke, the traffic built up and the coin collection started to pick up pace. The curious ones hung around, sipping a steaming cup of tea, and gossiping. Soon, a scattered group had assembled, the question raging across them was on the identity of the person.

The inevitable knowledgeable ones sprang up, each more vociferous than the other with his opinion.

"*Arre*, I know who this is!" The speaker was an oldish man, unshaven, clearly out for his morning ablutions but distracted by this unusual occurrence. The others around him looked curiously at him, a few urging him to reveal all.

"Yes, yes, I know… you know that Shyamlal? *Arre*, that vegetable seller across the street…? Don't you know?" The others looked at each other, unsure but eager for the delicious gossip. They urged the speaker on.

"I know it is him! I tell you, I saw him yesterday…" He looked around, pausing cleverly, drawing out the interest of his audience, then went on, hurrying a little when he saw a couple of his listeners losing interest and looking away at another similar group.

"I saw him yesterday, and he looked very ill! It must be him…" He concluded importantly.

One of the younger men snorted. "*Kya, chacha*[47]! So Shyamlal decided to die, lay down here and covered himself with that sheet, huh? And also placed those flowers? Huh?"

As the others started to guffaw, the knowledgeable one stomped off angrily, muttering they would all come running to him when he was proved right. This group then dispersed, some members merging with the other groups. In another group, the knowledgeable one proclaimed the dead person was a rickshaw puller who had been suffering from tuberculosis. He then went into much description of the suffering, the grim pathos of his family and so on, until someone asked him how did he know so much. Then his narration went into a kind of terminal decline and the people around drifted away.

However much the people stood around and speculated outrageously, no one dared to actually check the identity out by simply lifting the sheet. They baulked at that, superstition uppermost on their minds. Other people continued to drop coins there, the collection quite substantial by then and continuing to grow.

The first ripple in the till-then smooth situation occurred a little after 0600 hours. It was bright by then, huddles of people still around, speculation rife, when suddenly Mukund groaned. It wasn't much audible in the open though the few who were nearest did hear that but couldn't place its source. One or two looked at the covered form and were about to look away when all hell broke loose: Mukund raised a hand to scratch his belly.

The people looked on in horror, their attention drawn by a few coins tinkling on the road when Mukund moved his arm. They watched the hand scratch the belly then flop down again but this time it came loose from under the sheet and hung over the edge of the low platform, fingers curved but still.

---

[47] Literally, "what, uncle", here a derisive comment; *chacha* being a common term of reference for elderly men

Shrieks of fright filled the air as the people shrank back in horror, all wise words frozen. Only gaping eyes and open mouths ranged around. Before sense could regain her throne, the dead man let out a loud snore, gagged on his breath and hacked a terribly hollow cough, the whole "dead body" jerking in tune with that coughing. Then he made loud swallowing sounds in his throat and turned on his right, pulling the sheet loose and causing a mini cascade of coins to clatter on the ground. As terror mounted among the people there, it appeared the dead body was settling into another round of satisfying sleep. But that was not to be. All the drinking had apparently caused his throat to run dry and Mukund groaned again.

The curious were perhaps not feeling so curious any longer, just frightened out of their early morning skins, leaving them mostly speechless, excepting for a couple of people that appeared to have plans of keeling over soon. Early morning passengers, either entering the station or leaving it, paused, and stared in horrific fascination, barely breathing.

Then Mukund woke up. The people watched, hardly believing their own eyes, as Mukund groaned yet again and sat up. He was a sight to behold. Hair askew, eyes bloodshot and peering short-sightedly around him. His shirt was half undone down his front, the vest underneath filthy with sweat and dirt. He scratched his chest and looked around, clearly blown out of his mind on finding himself somewhere he had never, ever expected to be; it was plain that he was flummoxed.

At that moment, a cry rang out, sharp and clear. *"Murda jaga! Murda jaga!"*

As Mukund watched in bewilderment, people ran in all directions, the intrepid, the curious, the knowledgeable and the sceptic, all ran. Some stopped at a distance while the others disappeared either inside the station or well away from it. The cry of *"Murda jaga!"* continued to echo though.

Then Mukund looked down at himself, at the place where he sat, noticing the piles of coins around him, the few flowers and that damning white sheet. He gaped dumbfounded, scratching himself all over while trying to assimilate the streams of information his eyes were pouring into his still sub-par performing brain. His throat felt as dry as a mug of sun-dried sand, and he could now feel a humungous hangover coming on. He needed to drink water. Looking around, he spotted the public use tap located to one side and lurched towards that. A few people that were in the general direction scattered at his approach, some shouting *"Murda jaga"* still. Mukund looked at them and swore although no audible words escaped his mouth. He drank copiously from the tap, completely wetting the front of his shirt and vest and then staggered back to the spot where he had lain. The coins had his attention.

As he lurched back there, a stream of the choicest invective flowed from his now sluiced throat. Nervous laughter ringed him but from a safe distance. Surely, the people thought, this ghost was not really a ghost, not if it swore so colourfully and anyway, its feet were definitely touching the ground! But why take a chance? They stayed a safe distance away.

Mukund reached his spot and spread the sheet. Then he picked up the coins, slowly and deliberately, so as not to miss any, and put them in the sheet. Soon a pile gathered. Once he finished picking he made sure he had missed none, frequently looking up balefully at the people and keeping up the tirade. Most of the people were now laughing, most in relief and some at the absurdity of the situation.

Ramsaran had been present when Mukund had gotten up and he had followed the entire sequence of events from then, and had also sent information to Manab through another porter. Manab made a quick visit and observed from the inside the main entrance, smiling to himself, before returning to his office where he was handing over to the morning shift ASM.

Meanwhile, Mukund completed his coin collection and paused to patiently count the stack. Apparently, he had a good pile for his swearing ceased as he tied up the coins in the sheet and hefting it up on his shoulder, staggering a little, he walked off, out of the station premises. The people slowly dispersed, and normality regained her vacated throne to begin a normal day at the station.

Manab learned later from Ramsaran that Mukund had immediately gone off to a local *theka*[48] and started his binge from that early morning with the money he had collected while he had lain "dead". While this was not quite the outcome that he had anticipated, the overall incident did serve some purpose.

When Mukund finally came back to work the following day, he apologized profusely, promising to never commit such a gross lapse in duty. While a formal complaint was logged, Manab took pity on him and put it down as ill-health caused absence from duty. Mukund actually did not repeat such an incident till the time Manab worked at the Patna Junction station.

---

[48] Country liquor shop/ shack

6

Kanausi[49]

The train curved into a turn causing the wind to howl in through the open door of the third-class sleeper coach. The June sun was as pitiless as ever, the dry heat of May slowly giving way to humidity though rain was still weeks away. The rushing wind was thus a pleasure against the skin and a special relief for the spry but old woman squatting by the door.

Imarti Devi, for that was the old woman's name, kept mumbling to herself, more in anxiety than anything else. This business of alighting in time always terrified her; she couldn't read, her eyes were not what they had been a few years ago, and she had her bundles to get off too. She had to depend on her recognising the station based on familiarity and yes, that bench on the platform that had lost half its backrest to the rigours of time. And the not so kindly treatment of its users.

She had boarded the train at Kiul[50] after missing the passenger train she usually took back to her home near the hamlet of Bankaghat. The coach she had boarded was different she noticed, less crowded and people actually lying down in bunks. But she didn't pay attention, her mind on her twin worries: her need to get off at her station within time, and her cantankerous son who she'd need to deal with once back home. She kept to herself, studiously avoiding eye contact with any passenger who boarded after her, trying to squeeze herself into a corner. She certainly had the experience of

---

[49] Small, plain earrings

[50] A major railway junction in Danapur division of East Central Railway in Bihar

being shooed off trains and prayed she wouldn't have to fend off some TTE[51].

The stop had been only a couple of minutes and the train had soon started, gathering speed. Things quietened down, no TTE appeared; God certainly appeared to be smiling. She arranged her bundles and settled down to wait for her station to come by in a few hours.

Imarti Devi squinted out of the door, both hands gripping the handrails. Ah, there were the familiar structures of her station ahead up the curve the train had just taken. Those must be of Bankaghat. She glanced around her, inside the coach. All was quiet, no one bothered to look her way. All the better! She gathered up her bundles, still grumbling under her breath in anxiety, and returned to the door. The train should start slowing down any moment now.

Only it didn't. The train whistled briskly, long, and shrill, breaking through her thoughts. Imarti Devi was confused. Then, as the train continued to rush on, panic set in. The train was not stopping! What was she to do? The rushing structures of the station came closer and closer... and flashed by! In her panic, she missed the half-broken bench on the platform, faithfully confirming it was indeed Bankaghat going past. The guard at the station waved his green flag. But Imarti Devi noticed nothing. Sheer panic froze her.

The station whizzed past, the train implacable in its onward rush, whistles confirming intent of that. Imarti Devi snapped out of her daze with a start. She had to do something! She clutched her bundles... and jumped.

Manab had come over to Bankaghat station the day before, as he did every Monday early morning, to begin his three-days-a-week stint there. He spent the rest of the week at his base location station, Patna Junction. He had recently been given the additional responsibility of Bankaghat, a small station close to Patna, as well. While this tended

---

[51] Travelling Ticket Examiner

to disrupt his family life, he was blessed to have an understanding wife and he recognized this dual responsibility as another step in the growth of his career.

Bankaghat, being the small station it was, had just one day porter to support Manab. That day, he had just finished a hurried lunch when Madhav, that day porter, came running, his face wreathed in lines of worry, sweat streaming in the muggy heat.

"*Sahib*, there's been a terrible accident!"

"What? And where?"

His first worry was the Patna station: it was a very busy station and an accident there could have very serious repercussions.

"Bankaghat, *sahib*! A woman, cut to pieces!"

Manab knew he had to get there immediately and take charge; rail traffic would be stopped until the body had been cleared off the tracks, which was the rule. He ran along with Madhav who also informed him that this news had been brought in by a few villagers of that general area.

They came upon the spot soon, less than half a kilometre from the Bankaghat station. Usually desolate, now there were a couple of locals, gawking at the macabre sight. The sun was shining with relentless intensity and in that pitiless glare the scene that confronted Manab was indeed gruesome. Pieces of a body lay strewn across the tracks over a wide area, hardly recognizable as human. Blood and viscera splattered all over the place, flies buzzing over them. Bile rose sharply in Manab's throat and he vomited on one side, away from the scene from hell. He spat a few times and wiped his lips. Then he walked briskly up to one of the locals.

"Find a couple of sticks and keep any stray dogs away, will you?" He spoke with an authority that he probably drew from his diverse experience in dealing with uncommon situations. He looked at both the locals, indicating he wanted both to do what he wanted. The men nodded, clearly in awe of the "rail-*sahib*[52]". He then gestured at Madhav to accompany him for the grisly task at hand.

They began gathering the pieces of the mangled body and putting them to one side of the track. Manab had tied a *gamchha* over his mouth and nose, for there was a foul stench and the flies were infuriating. He retched several times during this while, and was conscious of the urgency to file the report and ensure traffic was restored on this line. When the pieces were gathered in he made up his mind to get going on that.

"Madhav, I've to leave here to submit the report of this accident, inform the GRP and signal the restoration of rail traffic. You're in charge of this place until the police get here and take charge themselves. Stay put!"

Manab had tried, over the next few days, to put the macabre incident behind him as best as he could. Shalin Singh, the GRP inspector, updated him of the status of the still ongoing investigation: The woman hadn't been identified, no name was known yet. Neither had there been any claimants for the body for two days and as there was no morgue available, the police cremated that as an 'unknown', which was the usual practice. Also, their enquiry indicated that the woman had boarded the Tinsukia Mail at Kiul station, mistakenly most likely, intending to get off at Bankaghat where the train did not, however, halt. Presumably panicking when the train whizzed past Bankaghat, she had jumped, with disastrous consequences. There was no question of any official compensation since she had not been a ticket-holding passenger and the responsibility of her unfortunate death was entirely hers. Sympathy, yes; compensation, no.

On the Thursday of the following week of this ghastly happening, as Manab was at his desk poring over some pending files at the Patna station, Ramsaran, the day porter there, knocked on the door.

---

[52] Lord of the railway!

"*Sahib*! There are a few villagers outside… they want to meet you…" Ramsaran appeared ill at ease.

"Eh? Who're they?" Manab barely paid attention, hardly raising his head from the files.

"*Sahib*…" Ramsaran's hesitation finally caught Manab's attention. He looked up.

"Yes, Ramsaran, what is it? Who're they? Speak up!"

The fellow sidled up closer. "*Sahib*, one of them says he's the son of that woman…" He wriggled his eyebrows meaningfully.

That made no sense to Manab. "Which woman?"

Eyes opened wide, Ramsaran gestured over his left shoulder. "That Bankaghat woman, *sahib*, the one who was cut into pieces!"

"Oh? A son?" He instinctively felt wary of such a sudden appearance of such a claimant. Where had this fellow been till now? "Anyway, send him in…"

"And the others?"

"Ask them to wait outside." Manab was clear he didn't want to crowd his office.

Ramsaran left and soon, a young man entered hesitatingly. He folded his palms together, clutching a *gamchha* between them.

"*Namaste*[53], sahib!"

"*Namaste*! What's the matter?"

"Er… *sahib*, um… my name is Bablu…"

"Yes, go on… Bablu?"

"*Sahib*, I am Imarti Devi's son…" He paused with an expectant look on his face.

Manab kept quiet though he had no difficulty in connecting this name to the as-yet-unidentified dead woman with Ramsaran's prior

---

[53] Traditional Indian form of greeting, often accompanied by bringing the palms together in front of the face or chest

information. He wanted this young man to say more so that he could understand the purpose of this visit so late after the incident.

"Okay, go on…" He kept his voice gentle.

Visibly uncomfortable, Bablu struggled to speak. "She's the woman who was cut down by the train…"

This phrasing sounded odd to Manab, it was as if the train had a malicious motive.

"It was an accident, Bablu, a very unfortunate accident," he said even more gently. Was it for some compensation that this fellow had come, he thought to himself.

Bablu looked away, then down at the floor. Was he wrestling with great sorrow, wondered Manab. Intuition told him that was not the case. If there was grief it was very weirdly demonstrated. He decided to take the initiative.

"Where do you live, Bablu?"

"Damariya, *sahib*…"

That didn't sound familiar to Manab. "Where is this?"

"*Sahib*, it's two *kos* from Bankaghat, beyond Kothiya *gaon*[54]…"

That gave Manab a vague placement for Damariya since he knew about Kothiya.

"Okay, Bablu, I understand where you live but tell me, why didn't you come earlier? The police had tried to find her family…?"

Bablu slapped his forehead and then proceeded to rub his eyes with the *gamchha*, covering his face. As Manab watched bemused, Bablu's shoulders shook, and a couple of gasps wracked his slight frame. Weeping? Manab was not somehow convinced this grief was real. What was behind this show? Gentler prodding brought out a disjointed story of Bablu and his mother having a fractious

---

[54] Village

relationship and that on that fateful day he had stormed off in the morning after a slanging match with her. He had returned home only after 3-4 days when his wife told him his mother hadn't come back home after she had gone out for her daily foraging for alms. Since their hovel was beyond the village and since he was still annoyed with his mother he didn't look for her right away. Another couple of days passed and then, when the annoyance had turned to fright at his mother's continuing failure to return, he went looking for her. Someone in the village told him that there was some hoo-ha about a woman being cut to pieces near Bankaghat station. And to cut the long story short, there he was now in his office.

In a manner of speaking, Manab felt some relief at connecting the dots of the unknown woman's background but there was a disquiet also building inside him, quite inexplicable.

"I'm sorry for your loss, Bablu… but it's too late now… the police couldn't locate her family and had to cremate her." Manab got up, a thought striking him.

"Come, let me take you to the police. They have a few of your mother's articles that you may take back…"

The question of not believing Bablu or doubting his relationship did not arise as it made no sense for someone to claim relationship when there was nothing to gain, neither compensation nor any precious articles as heirlooms.

"*Sahib!*" Bablu's tone gave Manab pause. He cocked an eyebrow and waited for Bablu to continue.

"Police?" There was a quake in his voice. Manab reasoned this could very well be the usual fear the poor sometimes had for any sort of authority in general.

"*Sahib*, please help! Could… you…?"

"You want me to get them for you?" Manab understood the implied request. "But you'll have to sign… affix your thumbprint on a document to get your mother's belongings."

Bablu appeared woebegone. Then, with a curiously dismissive gesture, he said, "But she barely had anything with her… *sahib*, actually it's her *kanausi* that are of any value…"

Manab stood stock-still. *Kanausi*? Those small earrings? Usually of gold… Good lord! He didn't recall seeing them mentioned in the list of items recovered at the site?

"*Kanausi*? How many?" For they were usually worn in pairs…

"Two, *sahib*, two pairs…"

Manab did some quick, tense thinking. He was pretty sure there was no mention of any earrings in the list of recovered items. So, if this fellow was speaking the truth, where did they vanish?

Meanwhile, Bablu spoke further, diffident yet clear enough. "And, *sahib*, in your hands everything would be safe, wouldn't it?"

The implication of which was not lost on Manab for a minute. He was accountable for this and if the earrings weren't found, he'd be answerable, and not just to Bablu but to the GRP and his chain of command upward. He made up his mind.

"Okay, Bablu. I'll check with the police and if the *kanausi* are there I'll have them returned to you. Meet me in a few days' time, okay?"

Bablu caught on to the "if". "*Sahib*, surely the *kanausi* are there? *Mai*[55] wore them all the time!"

Manab patted Bablu's back to assuage him and for his own burgeoning worries, in a manner of speaking.

"Don't worry, I'll do something…" And with that he managed to pack Bablu off. He stood at the door of his office, watching Bablu and his companions, a couple of villagers, walk away.

Manab didn't delay getting to the bottom of these mysteriously missing earrings. While small, they had the potential to harass his

---

[55] Mother

peace of mind and cost him a pretty packet, perhaps a couple of thousand rupees. Definitely not a very palatable state of affairs.

He quickly fetched the file that had the list of items recovered from the site of the accident. As he had suspected, there was no mention of those earrings. He thought back to that day, distasteful as it was. Had the *kanausi* been there they'd certainly have been in this list, of that he was sure. He had left Madhav in charge of that area. He'd certainly be the right person to crosscheck with.

He called for Ramasaran and when he came in, Manab asked him to find Madhav. Only then did he learn that Madhav had not turned up at work for last three or four days.

"He called in sick, *sahib*, the first day and no news since then!" said Ramsaran in answer to Manab's specific question.

"He lives in Phulwari Sharif, doesn't he now?"

"Yes, *sahib*," Ramsaran confirmed.

Now, Manab's mind was solely focussed on solving this mystery, he couldn't wait. But a round trip to Phulwari Sharif would be several hours. With a sigh, he resolved to go there the moment he got off that evening.

He went back to his files and other regular chores of the day, but his mind was continually tinkering with those missing earrings. Of course, there was always the possibility Bablu was lying, he couldn't completely discount that. But instinct told him Bablu wasn't lying. Sure, he had clearly appeared more anxious for them rather than the unfortunate death of his mother but that wasn't really his concern. To his mind, the matter was clear: If the woman… what was her name… Imarti Devi… had owned those earrings then they now belonged to her son.

Manab left promptly for Phulwari Sharif, with Ramsaran in tow, when his stint ended for the day at Patna station. They boarded a train and headed out.

After de-boarding at Phulwari Sharif, Ramsaran took Manab along to Madhav's house, a small dwelling on a mean little street. They found him sitting outside smoking a *beedi*[56], with not a sign of illness evident.

Madhav jumped up, concern writ large on his face, on the sudden appearance of Manab, someone he clearly had not expected to pop up at his home.

"*Sahib*!"

Before answering Madhav, Manab dismissed Ramsaran, asking him to return to Patna. Ramsaran trotted off, back the way they had come. And then Manab turned to Madhav.

"So, Madhav, how're you doing now? Health okay?"

There was a sheen of sweat on Madhav's face. "*Sahib*! You needn't have troubled yourself to come all the way here… you'd have just asked me to come over, I'd have met you…" He sounded worried. "Please come inside…" he stepped back inside his house.

Manab smiled. "I heard you're unwell, Madhav, and that you've not been coming to work for a few days… and I needed to talk to you urgently, couldn't wait, so thought of coming over myself."

"Yes, *sahib*, a bit of a fever… I should be able to join work tomorrow…" Madhav replied.

Manab came inside the house. He fancied he saw a veiled woman watching from behind a door further inside; possibly Madhav's wife.

Manab suddenly felt he wanted to get this over with soonest. He cleared his throat. "Madhav… that woman who was killed in that accident near Bankaghat… she's been identified. Her name's Imarti Devi, and her son had come today to meet me."

Madhav's eyes followed his every move. He nodded.

"Yes, identified. And, her son, Bablu, says his mother, this woman,

---

had two pairs of *kanausi*… and he wants them back. Now, I don't remember seeing them. Do you?"

Madhav shook his head immediately in denial. "No *sahib*! There were no *kanausi* at all! That fellow is lying!"

Manab was looking at Madhav steadily since he had come in; the sheen of sweat was quite pronounced though was accountable to the muggy heat. But he did appear shifty.

"Think about it, Madhav, seriously… did you miss them completely?"

"No *sahib*, not at all! I remember very clearly, there were no earrings!"

The over-eagerness rang false to Manab's ears, but neither could he assert otherwise specially since he himself remembered nothing. He looked at Madhav keenly, trying to see behind the denials. Madhav appeared unmoved despite the sweaty face.

Manab swung around abruptly. "Okay, Madhav. You get well and join back at work the soonest," he said and strode off. Madhav was too taken aback to respond to his sudden departure.

As he walked rapidly towards the station, Manab wondered what could he do next. The chief question to be considered, he felt, was: Did the earrings exist? As before, his instinct told him, insisted to be sure, that Bablu hadn't been lying. So, if that was true, where did they vanish? Could it then be Madhav?

He made a snap decision. The local *thana* was on the way to the station and he knew the *daroga* there well. He turned there.

Inspector Pandey, the *daroga*, was a large man with a paunch and a heavy moustache. He was there inside, holding court with his underlings, sipping tea. He jumped up on seeing Manab enter.

"*Arre dada*! What a surprise! This is really an auspicious occasion for us! Come, come, sit here!" The inspector exclaimed. He asked an underling to vacate a chair, and ordered special tea to be served to Manab.

The rest of the staff at the small *thana* went off quickly, giving them some privacy. Someone quickly served a glass of thick, milky tea.

"Yes, *dada*, tell me! Your coming here is certainly to do with something important… is it something to do with that accident where that woman was dismembered?" Pandey asked shrewdly. "You look a little troubled…?"

Manab sipped his tea, a sigh escaping him. "Yes, Pandey-ji, there is something I want to consult you for… yes, connected with that train accident."

He then ran through the whole episode, starting from the accident, the gathering of the pieces of that woman's body, the cremation, the sudden appearance of her purported son and then those missing earrings.

"Hmm… hmm…" Pandey looked thoughtful, pulling at one end of his luxurious moustache, as was his wont when thinking. Manab kept quiet, mulling over the main points himself of his narration.

A few minutes of quiet and then the inspector slapped his desk with one hand.

"*Dada*, you say you believe this son, this Bablu, about those earrings, right?"

Manab knew he was going out on a limb on this without evidence but he committed to going with his gut.

"Yes, Pandey-ji… I think Bablu is not lying."

The inspector slapped the desk again and got up with a start.

"Okay, *dada*, then let's go and visit this Madhav of yours…" He strode off with Manab hurrying after him.

"Pandey-ji, but I've already asked him!" He said as he ran to catch up with the fast moving *daroga*.

"Not in my style, you haven't!" was the cryptic reply.

They reached Madhav's house back in a few minutes, the evening darkness masking the dirty lanes. Madhav was still lolling around the front yard of his house. He spotted them at a distance and stood stock still, mouth agape.

As they reached close, Manab hailed him. "Madhav, we've come back…"

Before he could respond, the inspector strode up to Madhav and asked him, in a voice hard as steel, "Madhav? Tell me the truth!"

There was no preface, no introduction, no background. Just a question asked aggressively. There was panic on Madhav's face by now, his jowls shuddering, eyes opened wide in fright.

"*Sahib*! I don't know! I haven't done anything! I don't have those *kanausi*!" He was casting pitiful looks of appeal at Manab.

The next moment was perhaps the most unexpected. Without another word, Pandey swung his right hand across Madhav's face, slapping him so hard that the latter went sprawling on the ground. Manab flinched at the loudness of the stinging slap, shock coursing through him. Pandey stood over Madhav, a figure of intimidating aggression, moustache bristling. Manab was about to remonstrate with him, quite automatically, when there was a woman's wail heard from within the house and out she came running, tears streaming from her eyes, clutching something in her hands. She leapt over the sprawling Madhav and went straight at the feet of the *daroga*, grasping them with desperate fingers.

"Forgive him, *sahib*, forgive him!" She wailed. "He made a mistake… he was consumed by greed… he shouldn't have taken them from a dead woman…!"

And she dropped a small twist of paper at his feet which the inspector stooped to pick up. He didn't even open it. His expression changed to one of self-satisfaction as he dropped that into Manab's hands with a smile.

"Here, *dada*, here are the *kanausi*… check them for yourself… go on, check!"

Manab opened the twist of paper wonderingly and sure enough, there lay four small earrings. Quite inconspicuous plain rings, ordinary, but discernibly made of gold. The two pairs of *kanausi*.

The story was simple. When Manab had left Madhav with the gathered pieces of the woman's body, he had noticed the glint of gold in the severed head. Like his wife said, he was consumed by greed and literally the golden opportunity. He had ordered the two locals to go further out to keep dogs away and had then wrenched those earrings out of the poor woman's ears, confident they would not be noticed.

When Bablu turned up a couple of days later to check with Manab about the earrings, he got him to affix his thumb print on a stamp paper that declared that Bablu had received the four earrings in good shape and there were no further demands from him about his mother's death in that train accident.

And yes, Madhav lost his job.

7

Golden Fortune

Passengers of all shapes and sizes, in all possible hues and mostly in layers of winter clothing, were flowing out of the Gaya-Patna[57] passenger train standing on platform number 6 at the Patna Junction station, it's terminal stop. The usual controlled-chaos prevailed: *Coolies* trying to get in, early movers trying to get out, folks come to receive passengers trying to squeeze between momentary rivals, harried men and women tackling raucous children and stuffed-to-the-gills luggage while negotiating with *coolies*, and even a few vendors who had sneaked in with great hopes. In fact, quite the normal.

As the coaches slowly emptied, the railway cleaners boarded them, starting their sweeping and swabbing. Most had a piece of cloth tied around their faces protecting their nostrils from dust and occasional foul smell. The sheer volume of garbage generated in the course of a single trip is enough to make one wonder. Disregard and callousness make a potent combination. Cigarette butts, *beedi* tithes, and ashes of both, peanut shells, screws of paper, paper packets, bits of plastic wrappers, dirty rags, broken pieces of glass bangles, dry leaves and green, both used for wrapping some sort of food items, torn *paan*[58] leaves, bits of betel nuts, peelings of fruits, broken pieces and whole *kulhar*, tangles of hair, and tons and tons of dust and dried mud.

---

[57] The Gaya-Patna trains ran back and forth through the day as shuttles between these two stations

[58] Paan is a preparation combining betel leaf with areca nut and other masala, and sometimes also with tobacco. It is chewed for its stimulant and psychoactive effects. After chewing it is either spat out or swallowed

And of course, streaks and puddles of *paan* spittle, especially in the corners, besides occasional dollops of vomit. Only rarely did they find anything valuable or useful. The cleaners moved slowly, dusting, swiping, swabbing, and cursing occasionally, moving the veritable mountains of garbage from one end of the coach to the other and then packing them up in sacks.

One such cleaner, working with a younger fellow, in the general compartment that was third from the guard's brake van, was moving slowly down the length of it, sweeping a growing pile of trash ahead of him, and reached the seat numbered 41. Underneath, he spotted two medium-sized cloth bags, quite stuffed, one greenish and the other a muddy shade of brown, quite nondescript.

"Huh?" The sweeper looked up and around, as if he expected the owner to manifest there just then.

"What happened, *chacha*?" The younger man asked from behind him.

The older man gestured at the bags under the seat. "These bags… filled with… stuff…"

The younger man bent and dragged the bags out and started to open one.

The older man quickly bent down and held his arm. "No, Lalan, don't open it! The owner will come any minute to claim them!"

"*Arre chacha*, all have left! There's no one on the platform now… let's see what's there!"

And before the older man could prevent him further, Lalan pulled open the cloth string that held the handles together. Both looked into the bag… there were packets stacked tightly. Lalan then opened a packet. Sticky sweets, oozing syrup. Another packet, same finding.

"Bah, *chacha*! Only sweets!"

The older man quickly tied up the opened bag and hefting them up, started to walk away.

"*Arre chacha*! Where're you going with them? Let's eat a few sweets!" Lalan cried good-naturedly, breaking into laughter.

The older man smiled, carrying on walking. "I'll hand them over to the guard-*sahib* of this train for him to give them to the station master *sahib*…"

Manab had stepped out of his office for a quick break, a nice smoke, and a cup of hot tea. It was a cold morning, just around 1030 hours, the sun shining enough to make the wintry morning pleasant. The steady flow of work had been unceasing since the start of the day. There were problems of assignment, berthing, cleaning, staffing, departure timing, complaints… and a break for fifteen minutes would revive his energies for the next few hours again… or so he thought.

He still had the Bankaghat responsibility with him with the routine still the same: He worked three days at a time at each location, Monday through Wednesday at Bankaghat and Thursday through Saturday at Patna. While the pink bliss of his marriage was going strong, his career too was progressing well. His current boss, Mithilesh Prasad, a veteran of 25 years, was the station master and he tended to treat his ASMs with patience and humour. That suited Manab perfectly, the rigours of Bankaghat notwithstanding.

As he was returning after his break, which had proved agreeable, underscored by a couple of cups of rather delicious tea, Ramasaran accosted him.

"*Sahib*, I was looking for you…" he said.

Manab gestured for Ramsaran to fall in with him as he kept walking.

"What's it, Ramsaran?"

"The Gaya-Patna guard, *sahib*…"

"Eh? The Gaya-Patna train's, you mean? What about him?"

Manab usually maintained patience with Ramsaran as he tended to dribble information.

"*Sahib*, his name's Bhimsen... he's here to meet you ..."

Manab found a dark man with thick, greying moustaches and a respectable paunch waiting for him just outside his office room, holding two bulging bags.

"You're Bhimsen?" Manab asked him, motioning him to follow him into his office.

"Yes, ASM-*sahib*..."

"So what's the matter, Bhimsen? You wanted to meet me?" Manab seated himself behind his desk piled with papers and files.

"Sir, the coach cleaners Kalua and Lalan, were cleaning a general compartment on the Gaya-Patna. They found two bags under a seat..." He paused, looking expectantly at Manab.

"Bags? Of what?" Manab was already sifting through some of the papers on his desk.

With his tone implying complete mystification, Bhimsen replied, "Sweets!"

Manab looked up at this, and after a beat, asked, "Sweets? So?"

"Er... what to do with them? Should I inform the GRP?"

Manab put his pen down, and thought for a moment. General compartments did not have passenger manifests so there would be no way to contact the owner. Making a quick decision, he said, "No need to bother the GRP with such a petty thing. Keep the bags in this room. I'm sure that person will soon come back for them ... must have slipped his mind when he was getting off."

Manab then examined the bags cursorily, found them stuffed with sweets as reported and waved at Ramsaran to put them away in one corner of the room. Then he dismissed Bhimsen and Ramsaran and went back to his piled-up work, and in a few minutes, he was completely lost in there.

It wasn't until the next day, a Saturday, when he came back to work and saw a thick strand of ants in his office that he remembered the bags. The ants were running all the way from the bags of sweets in one corner of the room to outside from under the entrance door. He rang for Ramsaran right away.

"Ramsaran, get this cleaned up right now! And, did anyone come looking for the bags yet?"

A lugubrious shake of the head was Ramsaran's response as he readied to clean the mess up. A few minutes later, when it was done, Ramsaran came up to his desk.

"*Sahib*, may I suggest something?"

"Yes, Ramsaran."

"These bags… please take them home for safekeeping…" Seeing Manab raise his eyebrows, he hurried. "Yes, *sahib*, for one, we'll be free of these troublesome ants… and the other…" he paused, clearly seeking courage.

Manab didn't harry him, just looked at Ramsaran steadily until he spoke again.

"These are sweets *sahib*… the young lads here… may be tempted and swipe a few… cause unnecessary problems when the owner actually turns up… just suggesting, *sahib*!" he concluded ingratiatingly.

Manab held his silence. He was amused in part to hear that there could be intrepid souls around that could dare to pilfer a few sweets, and concerned in another for the owner could certainly kick up an issue if his sweets were stolen…

"Okay, Ramsaran, thanks for suggesting. Remind me in the evening when I leave for home to take them along for safekeeping. Send someone to fetch them from my home if the owner comes tomorrow to claim these bags. And come Monday, I'll be in Bankaghat… so you'll have to do the same then too, okay?"

And thus it was that Manab carried the bags home himself that evening to the surprise of his wife, Mita and daughter, Keya, who danced around obviously anticipating a treat of some sort. Manab ruffled her head affectionately and explained patiently to both mother and daughter those bags were not their property, but were rather there for safekeeping until their rightful owner came by to claim them. Mita placed them in her store room on a tray overturned within a larger tray half-filled with water which formed a barrier against ants. They soon forgot about them.

Monday dawned grey and cold and up with the sun rose Manab to leave for Bankaghat after a quick bath and a good cup of hot tea. He didn't feel up to breakfast considering the heavy meals of the previous day when his in-laws had come visiting. In fact, dinner had been so delayed that they had stayed overnight at his place. He was fond of them; Mita's parents were very affectionate and he was specially attached to his young brother-in-law, Abhishek, a college student, and sister-in-law, Mou, who was in class 7. Mita had in fact talked them into staying over for the next few days too as their winter holidays were on. Happy for Mita and Keya, Manab left early enough to get to Bankaghat by 0600 hours.

Two days later it was when the siblings were at their usual playful best, ribbing each other mercilessly that Keya slipped away for she had suddenly remembered those bags of sweets, and childlike, she wanted to have one just then. Only, when she went inside the store room, the bags were out of reach for her. A 4-year old's resilience was challenged and after a few minutes of puzzling over the problem, settled on doing what she had seen her father and mother do to reach higher shelves and lofts: get a chair. Off she ran to get one.

Now, senior ASMs rated 'railway quarters' more akin to bungalows and Manab's was specially so: sprawling and rambling, with an outhouse on one side and the rest of the house ringing a courtyard that was Mita's pride and joy, specially in the winters when the sun shone there right through the day warming her family and visitors, and provided the openness needed by her extensive kitchen gardens along a couple of it's sides. Mita had converted the outhouse into an extensive storeroom, the same one in which resided those unclaimed bags of sweets.

Mita and her siblings were in the same courtyard, enjoying the sunny warmth and their carefree time together. She hadn't noticed Keya's absence and was somewhat surprised to first hear a chair being dragged along somewhere and then seeing Keya pushing and pulling a wooden chair along the verandah with the evident intention of taking it down on to the courtyard. Mita ran to her to prevent an accident with the chair.

"Why are you pushing this, Keya? Stop it!"

Keya looked at her with pleading eyes. "Mommy! I want some of those nice sweets that Papa brought!"

Her lisping words were too cute for an outright refusal but Mita knew she had to cajole her child off those tempting sweets.

"*Beta*[59]! You know papa has asked us to look after them, isn't it? They're for his office… we cannot take any from them…"

Keya popped out her forefinger, small, cute and curved as a small child's. "Just one?"

Abhishek, who was only a few feet away, scoffed loudly at this denial by Mita. He was the child's *mama*[60], a relation meant by definition to spoil children.

"C'mon, *didi*[61]! *Jiju*[62] will not notice one measly sweet missing from all those boxes!"

He strode off into the storeroom, leaving the rest gaping after him.

"Abhi…" Mita then stirred up after him, intending to prevent the taking of any sweet out. Mou and Keya followed after them.

---

[59] Child; children are often spoken to with that as a loving prefix or suffix
[60] Maternal uncle
[61] Elder sister
[62] Sister's husband

A mildly sour smell assaulted their nose the moment they entered the storeroom. Abhi and Mita both stepped up close to the rack and sniffed loudly at the bags. Yes, there was a distinct sour smell emanating.

"They're spoiling!" Mita cried. She understood and appreciated the responsibilities that Manab shouldered and realized this could prove to be a bother for him. Her immediate concern had changed to trying to save the rest from the spoilt ones for surely not all could have spoiled?

She picked the bags up and came out to the courtyard intending to place them on the large multipurpose table there.

"What'll you do, *didi*?" Mou asked.

"I'll try to find the ones that are spoiling and throw them away… Possibly not all sweets are bad!"

So saying, Mita took all the packets out of the bags, sniffing at each packet and setting those that smelt off to one side. Of the thirty or so identical packets in total packed with the same type of sweets, it appeared there were 6 or 7 packets that seemed to be the offending ones. Out of sheer curiosity Abhishek opened one of these to inspect inside. Gooey sweets smelling a bit off. Mita picked another packet and opened. She picked one sweetmeat up and smelt it, her nose curling involuntarily, when her eye fell on something shining within the packet in her hands.

Shining?

She dropped the sweet in her hand and poked deeper inside. By that time both Mou and Abhishek were poring over her shoulders, wondering at Mita's amazed expression. Keya stood quiet, wondering what was keeping her *mama* from giving her one sweet as promised.

Mita moved a sweetmeat that was covering the shining object underneath, and stood with her mouth open in a perfect 'O'.

"What is this, *didi*?" Mou asked in hushed tones.

Abhishek joined her with a grunted "Huh?"

For staring at them was a golden biscuit. The object was rectangular, shining dully, and was somewhat larger than a standard glucose biscuit commonly available in the market. Mita picked it up in her hand and turned it over. Roughly etched on the opposite side were the words, "Gold" and "999.9".

She had yet to grasp this when Abhishek exclaimed, in a quiet tone though, "*Didi*, there's another beneath that one!"

Sure enough, there gleamed another one, a twin of the one Mita held. Abhishek took it out of the packet and turned it this way and that. It was identical to the first one, with the same words etched on one side.

All of them looked at each other, the same thought striking them simultaneously: Were there more?

The three of them started ransacking the packets of sweets with frenzied fingers: Open, rummage, put aside. Keya stood by, quite ignored in their excitement. They soon ran through all the packets in both the bags, but found no more of those gleaming bricks. The packets stood haphazardly, many sweets bore stark evidence of rough handling and their fingers were knuckle-deep in sticky syrup.

Mita realized she had been holding her breath for quite a while. She exhaled loudly.

"Okay… we have two gold biscuits. What do we do now?" It was almost a rhetorical question.

"Do? Nothing! We are rich!" Abhishek's face was wreathed in smiles, eyes aglow with excitement. And he started a wild dance holding the two gold biscuits in his hands and soon Keya joined him, little knowing what was all the hullabaloo for but enjoying the moment of madness. Her happy shrieks filled the air, while Mou started laughing and slowly Mita too, laughing for their joy.

"Okay, okay, you idiots, enough! Listen… we need to put the packets back together properly!" Mita brought them back to the present.

Abhishek grumbled a little, more with the intent of ribbing his elder sister saying over and over again they needn't work ever again with this golden fortune in their hands. After a while, they put the packets of sweets back in the two bags, remembering to discard those 6 packets that comprised the spoilt sweets. But they did not put the gold biscuits back.

Once the bags were packed up they stored them back in the storeroom as they were before, then washed the biscuits clean of all the stickiness. They sat around the table on the courtyard, even Keya joining them there.

"The question is, what do we do?" Mita opened their 'meeting'.

Abhishek's voice rang with certainty. "These are ours, no question about that, right?"

Mita shook her head categorically. "You can see someone put them deliberately with the sweets… knowingly. So whoever comes back for them will also expect to find the biscuits within."

Abhishek was quiet for a moment, considering her words. Then, defiantly, he said, reiterating, "No! No way are we going to return them! We found them and we'll keep them!"

Instead of arguing with him, Mita thought of diverting their attention.

"But don't you want to know how much these weigh? Only then can we know their value!"

Mou jumped in. "Yes, *didi*, lets weigh them!" Her eyes sparkled in anticipation.

Abhishek also turned his focus on that. He picked both the biscuits, screwed up his eyes and concentrated on his right hand that held them, gently moving it up and down.

"M..mmm… I'd say about 400 grams…" he pronounced.

Mita exclaimed in disbelief. "No way! Give 'em to me!"

She went through the same pantomime as her brother and then said,

"No more than 200 grams!" She looked at Abhishek. "You've no idea!"

Mou also tried her hand at it and came up with 300, just to even things up. They were in a quandary.

"Do you have weighing scales, *didi*?" Abhishek asked finally.

"*Arre* no!" Mita replied. "Though I can guess…"

They argued among themselves on what could be the best way to get the weight accurately without actually taking the biscuits to some jeweller… which would be very risky. Gold biscuits were completely uncommon for people like them to possess.

After a few minutes, Abhishek suggested they weigh them against something else and then he could take that to some grocer and weigh it… a roundabout method but feasible enough.

"Okay, we'd do that… but weigh with what? In the absence of a scale…?"

"In your hands, *didi*, just like you did now! You can feel the weights in both your hands simultaneously and surely you can sense when they're approximately the same… right?"

"Okay… what should we weigh them against then? Should I get some rice?"

Mou spoke up. "You won't be able to hold 300-400 grams of rice in one palm, *didi*!"

"That's true, *didi*… something that will be denser and will fit in your palm!"

Mita thought for a minute. "Okay, let me get my pot of coins that I save… those coins should do, right?"

They agreed that might do the trick. So the coins were brought out and Mita then held a small pile of coins in one hand and the biscuits in the other and concentrated hard, gently swaying one and then the other… adjusted a couple of coins… until she felt they weighed the same.

Then she handed them over to Abhishek, who went through the same motions, added another coin, and then pronounced satisfaction. Then he asked Mou to do the same. While Mou was doing this a thought struck Mita.

"Keya! Run *beta* and fetch Papa's paperweight from his desk inside!"

As Keya ran inside to do her bidding, Mita brought a stainless-steel plate from her kitchen. When Keya returned with the paperweight, she placed that on the table and after a few attempts balanced the plate on it. By then Mou and Abhishek were looking on with wonder.

"Now give me the coins and the biscuits…"

She took them and placed the biscuits on one side—the plate clattered down on that side—and then stacked the coins on the opposite side, and after several trial and errors, she managed to balance the plate perfectly, the stack of coins now perfectly offsetting the weight of the biscuits.

With a triumphant flourish, Mita smiled. "There you are! Now we know exactly!"

"Bravo, *didi*! This is brilliant!" Both Abhishek and Mou marveled at her simple solution.

Abhishek then went out to get the coins weighed and was back in less than fifteen minutes from the nearest grocer. The weight was 250 grams exactly. With that information in place, there was a stunned silence. As long as they were arguing and *doing* something, the value had seemed somewhat distant. Now…

"I think I read somewhere that gold is now sold at about three thousand rupees for 10 grams… which means…" Mita paused, wild surmise in her eyes.

"That's 75,000 rupees straight!" exclaimed Abhishek. His earlier glee had yielded to amazement.

The siblings were hushed into an awed silence. That was indeed an awful lot of money and suddenly, Mita was terrified. Even Manab was not home!

"What shall we do *now*?" Mou asked in a small voice.

"*We* will do nothing. Your *jiju* will be back tomorrow morning. He'll do what's needed." Mita emphasized the first pronoun.

As Abhishek made to protest, Mita spoke firmly, unwilling to brook any defiance.

"No, Abhi, no arguments! This is beyond us, involving enormous sums of money… I will not take any more risks!"

With that, before any more protests could be made, Mita swept the gold biscuits up in her hand and went off to lock them in her steel almirah.

They passed the rest of that day with excitement, fear and worry combining to keep them feeling restless until they fell asleep that night.

When Manab reached home early the following morning, barely 0500 hours, Mita was already up. The rest were fast asleep. A wave of relief coursed through her upon seeing him.

"Oh, thank God you're back!" Mita exclaimed, the tension in her voice alarming Manab, who dropped his bag and held her by her arms.

"What happened? Is Keya okay?" Mita's worry had conveyed itself perfectly to Manab.

"Yes, yes, she's okay… everyone's okay… it's not like that… something else…" Mita realized she had managed to scare Manab by her behaviour.

Manab appeared puzzled. "Then…?"

Mita took a deep breath. "Come inside…"

In their bedroom, she took the biscuits out from her almirah while Manab waited impatiently. She thrust them into his hands.

Manab gaped at them, struck quite speechless. He turned them this way and that, noted the etchings unseeingly. Finally, he recovered speech, well, sort of…

"Wha… whe…" His eyes were far more eloquent.

"You remember those bags of sweets?" Mita asked gently.

And then she recounted the story in complete detail. Manab listened without interrupting, his expression growing grimmer every minute. When she ended her narration, he asked her grimly, "There were just these two biscuits? You thoroughly went through all the packets?"

"Yes, just these two… we looked through each packet."

"Hmm. And Ramsaran never asked for the bags all these 3 days?"

"No." Mita had picked up the seriousness of the situation from Manab's tense body language.

"Okay. Come with me." And he strode off towards their storeroom, biscuits in hand.

Pointing at them, he asked, "Which bag did you find these in?"

After a moment's pause, Mita picked the greenish one. "That one," she said.

Without another word, Manab took that bag out and half emptied it of the packets. He picked one at random and opened it.

"You said the biscuits were placed somewhere in the middle of the packet, right, Mita?"

"Ye…es," she said, her brows knitted in concentration, pointing to a spot in the middle of the box.

Manab placed the biscuits there and put the sweets back then shut the lid, placing it back in the middle of the bag and stacked the rest of the packets over that one. Finally, he tied the string and placed the bag back on the rack.

Then he stood, arms akimbo. Manab cursed himself for not having examined the packets thoroughly himself before sending them over to his home, amongst his family… exposing them to needless danger. He knew gold smuggling was rife and the smugglers were very dangerous people, capable of deadly violence… he remembered Maya Devi from some years ago, when he used to be based in Mokameh[63]. Wasn't it likely that those men would be desperately looking for their gold by now? Surely, they wouldn't take that long to track the missing bags down to his house? And then…?

Manab shuddered inwardly, then composed himself. He saw Mita looking at him worriedly, possibly more concerned by his grim demeanour than any realization of their danger directly.

He smiled with an effort. "Don't worry, Mita. I'll take them back to the station today. Their owner will come by any day and we'll put this behind us, okay?"

The first thing he did upon reaching his office at the Patna station was to call for Ramsaran.

"Ramsaran, the owner of those bags," he pointed at them, placed back in the same corner of his office as before, "hasn't he asked for them all these days?"

"No, *sahib*, none has come till now…" Somehow Ramsaran guessed Manab was a little worried. Must be those sweets spoiling, he thought.

"Okay, but keep a lookout for anyone looking for these bags." He dismissed Ramsaran.

None came that day either but the following day, when Manab's worries had increased though he was also happy that the bags were out of his home, Ramsaran hurried into his room just before lunch.

"*Sahib*! There're a couple of men outside looking for those bags…" He appeared scared. "Very rough looking men, *sahib*… and they

---

[63] The Locked Waiting Room, story #4

correctly described the bags when I checked as you had asked me to…"

"Hmm. Okay, give them the bags."

As Ramsaran left with the bags, Manab got up from his seat and walked up to the door of his office, checking if he could see those men. His eyes followed Ramsaran. Soon, he saw two men lurking a short distance away, trying unsuccessfully to meld into the midday crowd. They had large shawls wrapped around their torsos, almost covering their faces with them. Nodding briefly at Ramsaran, they walked swiftly away with the bags. Manab slowly walked back to his seat, nodding to himself.

About a couple of hours later, Ramsaran came unbidden to Manab's office, his expression completely puzzled.

"*Sahib*! Lalan, the sweeper, found all those packets of sweets discarded outside near the garbage dump… All of them have rotted… Lalan checked… they should've come earlier for them!"

"Yes. I am sure… been many days now, isn't it? Almost a week…"

But they must have extracted those biscuits, he said to himself. He heaved a deep sigh of relief.

8
The Strike

"Dada!"

The voice reached Manab before the speaker appeared. He of course recognised the voice: Shalin Singh, the GRP inspector now based in Danapur. What was he doing here, Manab wondered as he got up from his seat in his office where he, as usual during the night shift, was poring over files that he seldom got a chance to clear otherwise.

He was walking out when Shalin entered, beaming, with a large earthen pot, tied with pink ribbon, in his hand.

The moment he saw the pot, Manab remembered. Shalin had been recently blessed with his second child, a daughter, and he now must be on his way back to Danapur to re-join work.

"Arre, dada! You forgot, huh?" His smile wouldn't dim.

Manab accepted the pot, heavy with *Gulab Jamun*[64], the specialty sweet from Shalin's home town of Sitamarhi, and placed it on his desk, then he hugged him and slapped his back in congratulations.

"Well done!" Manab said with a wicked glint in his eyes.

Shalin's eyes widened for a second then he started to laugh louder, caught up in the humour of the moment.

Then, after their laughter subsided, Manab asked, "So, what're you doing at Patna Junction station so late…? 1230 hours? What's going on?"

---

[64] Sweetmeats, dark brown in colour, dipped in syrup, famous through the country

"I'll tell you all… but let's get some tea, *dada*… that shack outside the station is still serving, just saw… c'mon, *dada*!"

Manab gave in with a smile, went back to his desk to put a couple of paperweights on all the masses of papers lying on his desk. As he squared things up a bit, Shalin explained.

"Actually, this is what happened… I's supposed to leave much earlier but a few of my college friends had come and you know how it happens to a new father… much fun at my expense… it got very late. And I had to give you the sweets… so I took a bus and reached here just now. Thought I'll take a train to Danapur to reach there early morning…"

"Oh, I see… I's wondering at this late hour…" Manab had taken the precautions he wanted and they were about to leave when the Control phone on his desk rang, sharp, shrill. He went back to take that, Shalin following.

"Hello! Patna Junction here… Control?" Manab said. A moment later, he exclaimed loudly, "What! When?" His eyes were open wide, the last couple of words exploding out of his mouth.

Shalin, a sharp man, asked, "*Dada*? Jehanabad related…? What's happened?"

Manab dropped the receiver into the cradle with a shaking hand. He looked at Shalin, unseeingly, a stricken look on his face.

"Ye..es… Jehanabad! Dinkar… Dinkar Prasad…!" Manab faltered, his shock slowly mirroring in Shalin's expression as the latter looked on at him.

Jehanabad is a small town about 45 kilometres south of Patna, and headquarter of the Jehanabad district. Jehanabad railway station serves as the main railway access point for the town and is a part of the Danapur division of the East Central Railway.

The Station Master, Dinkar Prasad, had been posted there for a little over a year. A veteran with Indian Railways, he was a stickler for cleanliness and efficiency, often running his team hard towards achieving those objectives. Like all station masters, he was a member of the All India Station Masters Association and great friends with Manab, though older than him by quite a few years. A man of medium height and darkish complexion, he was clean shaven and wore glasses around the clock. He was married and had one son, a stripling of mere 18 summers.

When he arrived at Jehanabad and took charge, the chief eyesores that bothered him no end were the local liquor shacks that had sprung up around the station, in fact within the station premises, around the portico. There were four of them, each a ramshackle, really, but they had been in existence for close on five years and did roaring business. The general stench of liquor and the consequent drunken behaviour of its patrons combined to drive Dinkar Prasad up the nearest wall. Such an ugly entrance to his station disgusted him and a few months into his tenure there, he made up his mind to drive them out if not shut them down altogether. And to his annoyance, he found out that there had been passenger complaints lodged over the last several years though no action had been taken. He wrote to his superiors, the Divisional managers in Danapur, sought and got their concurrence on acting against them.

His staff tried to dissuade him since the owners of those shacks were local criminals with too much dirty money in their hands. That they could be genuine risk to their lives. Dinkar had given them a patient hearing then told them in his mild-mannered way, "You don't worry. I'll deal with them personally, will request them a few times and if I fail in that approach, I'll think of a different way."

True to his words, he met with the gents that ran these shacks. The biggest of these was one that was also the oldest, situated flush next to the western boundary of the station, only a few steps from the entrance. It opened for business early in the morning and ran packed till it shut down much after midnight. Its patrons could be found all around and sometimes even inside the station; drunk, disorderly, and fouling up the premises with vomit, stench, and streams of abuse. Dinkar Prasad decided to target this one first. His meeting went something like this, as he had narrated later to Manab with great hilarity:

He had gone along with a porter to the liquor shop and requested to meet the *maalik*[65]. Such a request was unheard of and the surprise probably caused a burly, unshaven lunk of a man in a surprisingly clean white shirt to come out.

In barely understandable diction, that man asked, "Whaddya want?"

"I'm Dinkar Prasad, the Station Master at Jehanabad station., newly posted here. I've a request for you, please."

Such language was as surprising. After goggling for a bit, the burly guy, probably lacking the support of the roof of his mouth, tried his hand at replying.

"Whatisit?" It sounded to Dinkar that surprise had spurred the words out.

Dinkar slowed down his own speech.

"I. Have. A. Request."

The lunk made a noise in his throat that could have been a gentle request to make the request. Or at least that is how Dinkar decided to take it.

"I request you to please move your liquor shack to some location far from the station. The drunken people create a lot of problems for us, and the passengers. This will end if you can please move."

There was a momentary silence. The man stared, incomprehension oozing from every pore. Then he stomped off inside, shaking his hand in Dinkar's face. Dinkar stood a while longer, irresolute, wondering if he should stand there longer or return. The porter was making mute gestures, appeal in his eyes, for them to go back. Just when he was about to turn back, another man emerged, in a

---

[65] Owner

kurta-pyjama, gold chains hanging around his bulging non-neck. He had a pock-marked face, and terribly stained teeth—possibly thanks to *paan*—visible through a grimace or a smile that was hard to determine.

He stood close in front of Dinkar with his feet planted far apart, arms folded across his chest.

"What are you saying, station master?"

Dinkar made his request again, more politely. The man listened, his eyes unblinking. Then he spoke.

"Can't be done. This is my business and it'll remain here, don't worry your head with these things, station master… you'll get used to it."

With that he just turned around and went back in. Dinkar stood, nonplussed. Then he too returned to his office. Mission unaccomplished.

His experience with each of the other hooch shops was no different. No one agreed and one of them, the one that ruled the roost on the eastern side of the station, was downright abusive, spitting *paan* spittle and invective in equal measure. At one establishment he was hustled out by a burly doorkeeper while being screamed at by the owner from inside.

Dinkar was not the one to give up after one attempt. He made another round, or at least he attempted to, but he was not let within yards of the places, musclemen muscled him away. Thwarted in his good-cop approach, he decided to rack it up a notch. He went to the local police. It wasn't a particularly happy experience. They listened to him, sympathised with him and were free with advice, which boiled down to the quaint Indianism, "kindly adjust".

Dinkar was very annoyed by this attitude. On being asked, the SHO told him those shacks were really run by the pawns of very powerful criminals who even nursed political ambitions. That was the chief hurdle, Dinkar realised.

Then?

The SHO, a kindly man, tried to persuade Dinkar to look the other way. He advised him to depute a couple of porters to shoo drunkards away from the station premises and let things be. Amazed into silence, he left there soon after.

Then, about a month since he started this effort, a bunch of goons—clearly so by their looks—walked into his office unannounced while he was discussing some matters with his ASM, Asif. They were led by the same gent who had met him at the first shack, the one wearing *kurta-pyjama*. Even now he was dressed the same way, and his stained teeth were as visible through the grimace-or-smile-cannot-be-said expression.

He opened the conversation, if you'd call it that, thus:

"Rail-*babu*, one thing I'll say only once. All this *naatak*[66] that you're doing, stop it. Our shops will not close, okay? And if you push further…" he dropped his voice to a silky whisper. "I'll take no responsibility… you get me?" His eyes, red-rimmed and angry, glared at him.

Dinkar was mild-mannered but his streak of stubbornness was inflamed. Despite his exasperation, he kept quiet, resolving within to not give in.

Provoked by his continuing silence, the man ran his hand through his short-cropped hair as if trying to calm down. Then focussing on Dinkar again, he barked, "Understood?"

Dinkar nodded, calmly, deliberately not speaking. The goons left soon after this, the goon-in-chief unbending a little on getting an acquiescent nod from his quarry.

The next thing he wanted to do was to seek an appointment with the District Magistrate of Jehanabad, Sushil Yadav. Since he had earlier brought up the matter of these hooch shops with his divisional seniors at Danapur, he turned to them to create an opportunity to

---

[66] Literally, theatre. Here, theatrics

meet the DM. As it turned out in the next couple of weeks, he got his chance through a direct approach.

The DM, a young man probably in his early thirties, was far more understanding and supportive of the need for the removal of those liquor shacks. Like Dinkar, he too had been recently posted here and seized on this opportunity to clean things up.

A few weeks later, two vans of armed GRP constabulary alighted around the station and simultaneously charged the four liquor shacks. Because they were really shanties, bamboos, sackcloth, tin sheets, and rope-cots, rickety and just about functional, the policemen were done demolishing them in less than an hour. The patrons were mostly frogmarched to vans, some were given the benefit of one end of the policemen's *lathi*[67] but the men who ran the place mostly managed to escape, making particularly good use of the sackcloth.

So, the deed was finally done. The shacks were demolished, the drunkards had no reason to crowd around there any longer and the station could be cleaned up with the reasonable hope of it staying clean thereafter.

Dinkar Prasad was a happy man, with a righteous sense of achievement. His staff looked up to him with some degree of admiration, the locals considered him to be a really brave man and his seniors were very impressed with his determination and commitment. He got quite a few verbal commendations from them and glowed with justifiable pride. When he narrated the entire story to Manab, the latter was deeply impressed but voiced his disquiet that the promoters of those hooch shacks were still free. He urged Dinkar to be careful who waved away those worries, assuring Manab that their backs had been broken, for after all, where would they be getting their money now?

As Manab learned later, less than two months from that time, it was actually proved that those promoters' backs were not quite broken.

---

[67] Long batons used by policemen to quell violent crowds

That same evening when Shalin Singh came with his pot of *Gulab Jamun* for Manab, there was a rude knock on Dinkar's railway quarter's door. Dinkar was home and just having finished his dinner, was pouring himself a glass of water from the pitcher. He could see the door from where he stood. His son, Madan, that youth of 18 years, opened the door. Three men barged in, the first one shoved Madan hard, sending him sprawling on the small courtyard, while two men converged on Dinkar. All three wore long *kurta* and had their faces covered in *gamchha;* only their eyes were visible.

One of them shouted roughly, "Dinkar Prasad? Rail master?"

Dinkar's mind was in a whirl. Who were these men? His son was sprawled on the floor, trying to get up... why were these men shouting? His wife was screaming in the background he imagined. He felt disoriented.

"Hu...h?" he stammered.

The first man suddenly took out a handgun and shot him twice in the chest. Dinkar collapsed without a sound, like a sack of potatoes that's been suddenly undone. While Madan clambered up, the man who had shoved him reached forward and slapped him, throwing him back down on the floor. Then with a few shouts of warning to leave them alone, they left as quickly as they had rushed in. It was all over in less than two minutes.

"What happened, *dada*?" Shalin's voice was filled with concern. He held Manab, who appeared shaken, by his shoulder.

"D...Dinkar... he's been shot! In his h...home!"

Shalin helped Manab sit down, then gently asked him to tell him what he had been told.

Manab fought to get a grip on himself; his shock manifest. He took several deep breaths and gulped down some water.

"Seems some people crashed into his home a short while ago and shot him twice in the chest... he's been rushed to the hospital... but..."

"He was still alive then? *Dada*? What're they saying?"

"Don't... don't know... Control couldn't say any more... I'll... I'll find out... maybe the ASM there will know more?"

He dialled Jehanabad station's number right away. It rang a few times then someone picked.

"Hello?"

Manab recognized the voice.

"Asif, is that you? What is the news? I just got a call from Danapur Control about Dinkar-ji..."

"Yes, *dada*, this is Asif... Sir... he... he's dead... they couldn't do anything, he... he was too badly injured they said... just now, just now..." Asif was distraught.

"Oh..." Manab was speechless. He dropped the receiver back and sat down again, his head in his hands.

Shalin had overheard Asif. He laid a hand on Manab's shoulder again in commiseration. He had also known Dinkar Prasad: a good, upstanding man.

A few minutes passed thus, both sitting quiet, staring into the distance, clearly in the grip of the situation. After maybe ten minutes, Shalin cleared his throat.

"*Dada*, what will you do next?"

Manab shook himself out of the stupor. "I... I don't know... not exactly..." He looked up at Shalin.

"The question to ask here is, why was he killed? Who'd murder him so... so brazenly?"

Shalin shook his head. "It is very clear, *dada*, there cannot be any other reason... it is certainly the revenge of the hooch makers... who else could it be? He had no enmity with anyone else! And, look at their audacity! They enter their victim's house with impunity and shoot dead their target!"

His voice shook with suppressed anger.

Manab had turned completely grim, his jaws grinding. Of course it wasn't anyone but those dratted hooch makers. The other thing that struck him forcefully was that he had been murdered when he was off-duty. He was aware that compensation was given only when a death occurred while on-duty. He explained this briefly to Shalin and then set out to do what he decided was the most urgent need under the circumstances.

With the idea that was burgeoning in his mind, he needed to get the important and influential personnel of Patna station on board. They were the leaders, secretaries, senior members, and the doers of both the railwaymen unions, as well as the members of the All India Station Masters Association, of which he was the national secretary. He needed them to be present so that a unanimous course of action could be determined.

Then, with Shalin watching over his shoulders, Manab started calling them one by one. When Manab explained the reason for calling them at that ungodly hour, they understood and most agreed to come over to the station to meet and plan for action to be taken. Each agreed that they would need to lead the charge to ensure justice for Dinkar.

There were a hundred and thirty-eight[68] stations in Danapur division, comprising important ones like Patna Junction, Mokameh Junction and a few other junctions, besides smaller ones like Jehanabad, Kiul, Buxar, even Danapur itself, and several others. His idea could deal a sharp blow to the usual somnolence in handling a critical situation like this. It would be far more effective if he could consolidate the entire division's will towards dealing with this outrage.

The union leaders and other important members started arriving shortly after Manab's phone calls. About fifteen people ranged around in his office by 0330 hours. After the initial exclamations

---

[68] Valid in 1989; now there are 146 stations

of shock at Dinkar's death, the single point agenda was to decide upon the best strategy to ensure compensation and justice for him and his family.

Satyarth Mishra, the rotund union leader, had been sleeping at home when Manab's call awakened him and he had reached first, principally since he lived quite close to Patna station. He was also forthright with his views.

"See, gentlemen, it is very clear why Dinkar has been killed. Because he cleared up those hooch shops. And who did he do that for? The Railways. So, to me, whether he died on duty or off, it was for something he did for Railways… so he must be compensated, his family provided for. Right or wrong?"

There was a chorus of agreement. The general sentiment among them was in complete alignment. Manab however wanted to get an agreement on the *action* they ought to take. He raised a hand to get their attention.

"Gentlemen! We're in agreement on the reason for his death. I say we decide quickly on what we must do therefore… decide now, and do now!"

Dhiraj Kumar, a fiery young leader of the other railwaymen's union, was swift with his opinion.

"We must do something that will grab their attention… something that will hurt them…" he looked everyone in their eyes.

Manab asked, "What would do that?" He too looked around, and particularly at Dhiraj, the query plain in his eyes. He was willing them to arrive at the decision he considered to be the most logical.

Santosh Anand, secretary of one of the unions, spoke up. "The common factor here is the railway." He paused, then he continued, emphasizing his point with an extended forefinger. "We have to stop all rail movement, all trains."

Shalin, who had been relegated to the background during this meeting, was taken aback. That was a seriously strong step, one that could be fraught with consequences. He waited anxiously for the group's reaction to this proposal while Manab breathed a silent sigh of relief for having herded the group to this decision.

Mishra, Dhiraj and another lanky union member, Bishambhar Gupta, jumped up in enthusiasm.

"Yes!" exclaimed Dhiraj and he was immediately supported by Mishra and Manab. "Yes, we must strike work… we'll not let any trains pass in this division… not until the authorities agree to our terms!"

Barring maybe one or two, everyone chimed in. Yes, they agreed, they would stop all train movements forthwith. The consequences would be very severe, impacting many passenger and freight trains. Losses could be significant.

Since almost the entire group was in favour of the step, it took very little to sway the dissenting members and by 0400 hours, they had a unanimous decision that Manab would present as such.

The next thing was to prepare a list of 'demands', which the authorities would have to accept before services could be restored in Danapur division. Manab asked a core group of four to work on this list. He took the responsibility of informing Danapur Control of their decision to stop all train movements. But before he did that, he called up a few of the bigger stations and spoke to the station masters there, informing them of the killing of Dinkar Prasad and their agitation plans so that they would be prepared when they heard of this from Control.

The Control phone is a hotline connection. Manab had to just lift the receiver to be connected to Control room. In measured tones, he explained that the unions and the station masters' association had decided to stop all train movements effective 0600 hours in Danapur division. It was natural that Control wanted to know the reason for doing so. They were sympathetic when Manab explained and then flicked the switch to instantly connect with all the stations in the division and broadcast the decision formulated by both the unions as well as the station masters' association: No rail traffic was permitted from 0600 hours. The Divisional Railway Operations Manager was informed as was the Assistant Divisional Railway Manager.

This meant all stations between Mughalsarai Junction at the western end and Jhajha station at the easternmost end, that made up Danapur division, would eventually cease working. Trains that were within that area would be able to travel till the point they would have signal to proceed after which they would have to stop and await resolution. Tempers would fray, losses accumulate and pressure to find a quick solution mount. At least that is what Manab and all his partners hoped would happen.

By then it was beyond the time for Manab to handover to the next ASM and go home. He called up home and told Mita, his wife, that he was not coming back just then and gave a summary of their decision. She too knew and liked Dinkar and his death came as a bruising shock, her heart going out to Dinkar's wife and son.

The fifteen-member agitation team that had come together despite their traditional differences were within his office still, continuing their discussions. Manab thought they ought to move out of there to a more neutral—'non-office'—place to continue with their planning. He proposed this, and the others agreed so they moved to the portico area. Ramsaran set up folding chairs there for the men to sit and resume their work. He also served tea and biscuits there.

Manab instructed Ravindra Sekhar, the ASM who was to take over from him at 0600 hours, to deal with the passengers who would arrive at the station to travel and find trains stalled. All station masters had been told to tell the real reason for their agitation and such communication would be made as necessary.

As the next couple of hours passed, more and more trains stopped at some station if they could manage it or wherever they had last got a red signal. Traffic started backing up on the tracks and anxious calls were arcing from point to point, voices raised in anger or panic or both. Meanwhile, Manab had arranged for some breakfast for his team and just as they were finishing that, Ravindra Sekhar came running to tell Manab that the DROM[69], Amitesh Sinha, was on the line, wanting to talk to him.

It was a brief chat on the phone. After listening to Manab, Sinha told him he would come over to meet with the agitating team and work with them to figure out the quickest way to resolve the situation.

The next couple of hours passed in a whirl. Close on 1130 hours, he got a call from the west cabin that a diesel engine was approaching from Danapur with Sinha as the sole passenger. Manab was expecting this and directed the cabin to let it berth on platform 1. Ten minutes later the engine stopped, and Sinha hopped off it, received by Manab, Mishra, Dhiraj and Santosh. Manab led them to his office and seated Sinha there and got Ramsaran to organize some snacks.

Sinha, a middle-aged gentleman with a professorial appearance complete with a strapped pair of glasses, listened patiently to the points that the agitating team put forward.

"I understand your concerns, trust me. But there are rules that will apply here… you understand?"

The others nodded. Mishra reiterated. "Dinkar was off duty and rules state that compensation can be paid only if death occurs while on duty."

Sinha cocked an eye. "Yes."

Manab spoke with emphasis. "But, sir, we must consider *why* he has been killed. He had no enmity with anyone other than these hooch makers whose business he derailed… and that was for the railway! So, isn't railway liable? Doesn't it owe him a decent compensation for laying down his life?"

Sinha sighed. "I can very well see your perspective… but these rules…" his voice trailed off.

---

[69] Divisional Railway Operations Manager

"Then I'm afraid, sir, that we cannot withdraw our agitation… not until there is a fair settlement for Dinkar Prasad," Manab said respectfully.

Sinha nodded and got up to leave. "You gentlemen keep me posted on developments. Speak to the ADRM[70] and DRM[71]. Meanwhile, I'm taking this engine to Jehanabad to meet Dinkar's family. We have to stand by them."

This reasonable tone and humane intent worked to defuse their rising tempers and in particular, of the hot-headed Dhiraj. They walked with Sinha to see him off.

Manab then told the others that he would call up the ADRM next and convey their list of what they were terming their mandatory demands. He walked to the union's office to check with the core group on articulating their chief concerns.

"Do we have the list ready?" he asked.

Bishambhar Gupta, who was a member of this group, brought the list to show to Manab. It was filled with scratched out words and lines, rewritten and underlined; it was difficult to read in that incoherence.

"Bishambhar, can we please have this cleaned up? Then let's discuss this before we present it to the ADRM, okay?" he suggested.

Next, he called the ADRM who was in his office in Danapur.

"Sir," began Manab. "We request you to please take action on this matter. The unions will not budge unless there is visibly some action taken and a fair compensation offered to Dinkar Prasad's family."

The ADRM, Bansi Lal, was a tough character, seldom given to giving in. As expected, he took a tough approach.

"We cannot have negotiations on such matters, Manab. The rules are very clear, and we cannot wish them away. Stop this agitation,

---

[70] Assistant Divisional Railway Manager
[71] Divisional Railway Manager

restore services forthwith and I'll see what I can do, that's all I can offer at this stage."

Manab kept calm, telling himself to be patient, that it was early days yet. Nothing would move swiftly. Then he spoke.

"Sir, I respectfully must tell you that both the unions and the station masters' association are in complete agreement. And you know this degree of unity is uncommon. No one will agree to restoration of services without something to show for it."

Mishra, who was standing close to Manab, and had overheard Bansi Lal's opening statement, jumped in and took the receiver from Manab's hand who let it go easily enough as Mishra was the leader of the larger union and had the experience of dealing with tense situations.

"Sir, this is Satyarth Mishra… railwaymen's union secretary. May I speak?" It was a mere courtesy extended and Bansi Lal knew that. He politely asked him to speak.

Mishra kept up the politeness though Manab had the feeling that the claws could be bared at short notice.

"Sir, the matter is simple. Rules must accommodate ground reality. Here the reality is Dinkar Prasad lost his life in the line of duty, whether he was at work or at home is immaterial. Therefore, he deserves compensation."

The ADRM tried a different tack.

"What is the compensation you propose?"

Mishra hesitated a bit and Manab took the receiver back.

"Sir, we will present a formal draft to you. And we'll explain our point of view in detail."

After a brief pause, during which time Manab overheard Bansi Lal conferring in hushed tones with at least two other men in the background, he replied, "Okay, I'll come over to meet you at Patna station. I'll try to be there by 1330 hours."

Manab thanked him politely and disconnected the call. They had about two hours to be ready for this crucial meeting.

By the time the ADRM reached Patna station, the same way Sinha had, it was almost 1400 hours, and most trains in Danapur division had come to a halt. Confirmation of that had flowed in from many places. The agitation was successful insofar as stopping trains was concerned; but would they achieve their objectives?

Manab and the others received Bansi Lal just the same way as they had Sinha. Bansi Lal was a dapper man, sporting a thin moustache that was mostly grey and a scowl that was often intimidating. Manab led them to the union's office instead of his own. It was a subtle message that the ADRM, an astute man, must have noted.

They sat around the table in the room, Bansi Lal on one side and the others ringed around. As before, Ramsaran was ready with tea and biscuits that he served swiftly and left.

Bansi Lal hitched his impeccably ironed trousers at the knees and crossed his legs while the others waited patiently. Then, he cleared his throat and opened the proceedings.

"Okay, gentlemen, I understand you wanted to make a formal submission of your demands in the unfortunate matter of Dinkar Prasad's death. Please, tell me."

It had been decided earlier among the agitation members that, being the senior most, Satyarth Mishra would lead the discussion from their side. The other union leader, Dhiraj, had also agreed to this, which was in itself a strong reflection of their unity of purpose. Thus, Mishra spoke in reply, extending a typed sheet to Bansi Lal.

"Here is our list, sir. I will read out from a copy."

Bansi Lal glanced at the sheet as Mishra put on his reading glasses to read from his copy in hand. Manab observed Bansi Lal's face and noticed the curving down of the corners of his mouth.

Mishra began reading aloud. "First, there has to be a fair compensation paid to his family for his death. The amount cannot be less than a lakh of rupees." He looked up, but Bansi Lal's face was entirely noncommittal.

"Second, an immediate disbursal of fifteen thousand rupees for his funeral needs." Bansi Lal's face remained impassive.

"Third, railway will have to provide employment for his son, so that their future can be safeguarded to some extent." The ADRM's expression did not change.

"Fourth, the killers have to be caught and punished. Railway must work with police to ensure this." Manab noticed a slight movement of the ADRM's head but couldn't decide if it was a nod or a shake.

"Fifth, sir, there has to be suitable and adequate safety provided to railway officials, especially those that are required to undertake risk." Mishra looked at Bansi Lal and then at his team members. Everyone was quiet.

After what was threatening to become a competition of silence, Bansi Lal again cleared his throat loudly. Manab's ears perked up.

"I will immediately sanction numbers two and three, gentlemen. Four… I cannot commit but I will certainly pursue with the police. But for numbers one and five, specially one, I cannot give any guarantee right away. Granting a compensation… of any amount… has to be according to strict rules. I hope you understand me?" He looked up from the paper in his hand, eyes flicking from face to face.

Manab saw Dhiraj's face reddening with anger and quickly laid a hand on his shoulder, quietening him for the moment. Mishra spoke up, his tone neutral.

"Thank you, sir, for immediately agreeing to two of the five points. I think we can support you for your position on pushing for the arrest of those criminals, too. However, the gravest issue here is number one. How can we leave that out completely?"

Dhiraj shook Manab's restraining hand off and spoke, his voice hard. "I find it impossible to understand how can some petty rule come in the way of doing what is right!" He fumed, breathing stertorously.

Bansi Lal looked steadily at Dhiraj, without a change in expression. He said evenly, "I'll try but this has to go further up for approvals and like I said, I cannot make any commitment now."

Dhiraj appeared ready to fly off the handle and again Manab put a restraining hand, firmer this time. Mishra too turned back to look at Dhiraj with a frown and a minute shake of his head.

Manab said, "Sir, I think we need to discuss amongst ourselves for a bit and then we can meet to finalize? Would that be okay with you, sir?"

Bansi Lal thought for a moment then nodded. Tactfully, he left the union office, saying, "Okay with me. I will take a tour of the station while you discuss. You will find me when you're done?"

Left to themselves, the team discussed the points and whether they could move forward or stick to their guns. Predictably, Dhiraj wanted no truck with partial acceptances and wanted to ride it out. Mishra was vacillating while Bhishambhar and Santosh considered their immediate concerns had been addressed, particularly the job for Dinkar's son, Madan. Manab tended to agree with the latter two. He addressed everyone.

"Listen, my friends," he looked everyone in the eye. Then ticking off his points on his finger, he continued. "We have to consider a few things that are of immediate concern. One, the funeral cannot be delayed for too long even if a morgue were to be used to preserve the body. The summer heat is vicious. Therefore, the fifteen thousand that we have an agreement for is crucial. Two, the job for Dinkar's son is an assurance in the long term. That is a big plus. Three, I think we must insist on petitioning the DM for his support considering he was instrumental in uprooting those hooch shacks. I'm sure we'll get his support. And four, I say we also insist that we get this agreement in writing from the ADRM."

He paused, holding their gaze, willing them to agree. "As for the other points, chiefly the compensation one. I'm not sure how long or how far we can push them… how long can we afford to wait?"

Dhiraj bristled again. "*Dada*, you've been stopping me from speaking… but what face will we retain if we cop out on the compensation point?"

Mishra nodded. "Yes, I understand that point only too well… we've staked our credibility on that point. I agree… but like *dada* is saying, how long can we wait? There are urgent needs *now*!"

Santosh spoke up. "Mishra-ji, but who have we staked our credibility with now? In our eyes only… and perhaps the division senior officers. But we have to act sagaciously, within the constraints that define our immediate problem!"

Manab nodded. "I couldn't have put it better, thanks, Santosh! Yes, my friends, we need the money and the job assurance now. And as for the compensation, I propose we launch an urgent charity fund drive across the entire division! Surely we can collect a reasonable sum for Dinkar's family?"

Even Dhiraj was taken in by that idea. He looked brighter. "Yes, we can do that for sure!"

The rest of the team soon fell in with that and fifteen minutes later, they were ready to get Bansi Lal back to wrap it up.

They were done in half an hour. Bansi Lal had briefly resisted giving anything in writing but Manab took him aside and explained that unless that was done, the union leaders would take a non-negotiable stance, stymieing all chances for an early resolution. When he extended that argument by pointing out their compromise on the compensation clause to just a statement saying effort would be made to secure approval for a just compensation, Bansi Lal capitulated. By 1600 hours, the agreement was typed and signed. The agitators had secured a victory… or at least a meaningful compromise that served their immediate needs fairly well.

Once the ADRM left, the team met and then set about informing Control about ending their strike which Control immediately broadcast to all relevant stakeholders and privately congratulated Manab and his team in having secured a swift decision that met most parameters. Manab also informed Sinha about this who also congratulated them. He said he would personally convey the news to Dinkar's family.

Almost twelve hours since the agitation had begun, services started to resume, the much-harried passengers starting or restarting their delayed journeys, and delayed freight resuming their interrupted trundling. Manab could go home only for a short time before coming back at 2200 hours to resume duties.

Postscript: Dinkar Prasad's funeral was well organized and concluded with the required dignity and sensitivity. His son, Madan, was given a class IV job in Indian Railways, based on his education levels then. He, of course, had the option of enhancing his education and taking his career forward. The District Magistrate, Sushil Yadav, lent his full support and force that enabled the police to round up the entire gang of hooch makers and charge them with the murder of Dinkar Prasad. Manab ran a very successful charity fund contribution campaign over a few weeks and a substantial fund was collected and handed over to Dinkar's grieving widow and son.

However, neither could an official compensation be secured, and nor could any special protection be arranged at stations for railway personnel.

9

The Accident

Sukhiya gazed deep into the steel tumbler, the amber liquid appearing like molten gold to his alcohol-sozzled eyes. He dipped a finger into it and then licked it off… hmm, that tasted wonderful. He giggled to himself. Life felt good now, the liquor sloshing inside gave off waves of bonhomie, an urge to do good to the world at large. He took a long swig and picked up his bottle for a refill. Ah, there appeared to be at least one good, large drink left still despite his steady drinking for the last hour or more. He peered at the chipped enamel plate for any of the peanuts left and patted it since his vision was quite blurry; there was none. With a sigh, he poured the rest of the liquor into his glass and looked around himself. He was in a shabby shack: a few benches, a table that bore countless signs of monumental torture over time, a naked bulb that shone with grim determination upon a few similarly sozzled men. He smirked, took a swig, and smacked his lips. Quite inconsequentially, he suddenly remembered it was the evening of *Vishwakarma Puja*[72].

The Patna-Gaya passenger berthed on platform 6. The driver, Phani, an amiable man just a couple of years away from retirement, leaned on the handrail outside the driving cabin of the engine and watched the usual tumult on the platform but his eyes were drawn towards the *pandal*[73] that stood a short distance away at the loco shed to the south of the platform. It was tall and very colourful with saffron

---

[72] Worship of the Hindu god of architecture, *Vishwakarma*. Credited with building *Dwarka*, Krishna's city

[73] A tall, conical, and elaborate tent, usually colourful, where such festivities are celebrated

flags fluttering on the top. That was the *Vishwakarma Puja* that the railway staff celebrated there each year along with the people that ran the various shops and outlets that dotted all the platforms and even outside. Music was blaring from a loudspeaker, some Hindi film song. Phani smiled to himself, wistfully, for he was much attached to these celebrations. He was a regular at these events, more social than religious, but he was unfortunately on duty that day. Railway rules prohibited the driver of a train to leave a train unattended. He was therefore unable to run over to the *pandal*, offer his *pranam*[74] and partake of some rather delicious *prasad*[75]. The gossip there with his friends would strictly be bonus. He sighed.

Manab was enjoying the twists and turns, the mandatory endgame villainy, sacrifices, and reunions in the Hindi movie "*Mohra*[76]" as it was winding down to its rambunctious end. Mita, his wife, was equally engrossed in the seat next to him in the darkened theatre. The music was loud, the dialogue-*baazi*[77] intense and the three 'heroes' were giving the deserved pasting to the villainous hordes. It was good fun! They managed to slip out for movies fairly often and tonight, being a night shift for Manab, they had caught up with this movie making waves that season. Manab flicked a quick look at his watch, perhaps another fifteen minutes to the end. He needed to visit the *Vishwakarma Puja pandal* at the station too; the organizers were expecting him. No worries, he had ample time to do that after dropping Mita off home for they lived ridiculously close to the station.

The Howrah-Delhi Rajdhani Express was approaching Patna Junction station. It was only a few kilometres away, about to be sighted by the Home signal, from where it would guide the train for

---

[74] Obeisance, to deities and/ or seniors

[75] Offerings made to deities, usually fruits and sweets but also other foodstuff, distributed without let or hindrance

[76] Literally, 'Pawn'; a popular movie that released in the year 1994

[77] While 'baazi' by itself means challenge, dialogue-baazi is the accepted term for intense dialogue exchange between principal characters in a Hindi movie where each would try to pull the rug from under the other's feet

its berthing at the upcoming station. The driver of this train, Sukamal Dastidar, a serious gentleman, was keeping a sharp lookout for the Home signal, his hand hovering over the starting gear. It was only a 5-minute stop at Patna Junction but Sukamal decided he wanted that cup of tea after all, one that he had refused some half an hour ago. He peered short-sightedly, anxious to spot the green signal. Ah… there it was. They would soon be berthing at platform 4. Being a regular on this route, he knew that platforms 4 and 6 were physically the same platform, longer than usual platforms, but logically separated by signal bifurcation. Two trains would be berthed along them. This posed no danger as the lines were different; line number 6 for his Rajdhani and the usual other train on platform 6 would be the 8 Patna-Gaya passenger on line number 8. Upon signal, he would veer the Rajdhani on the bifurcated line, entirely avoiding the 8 PG.

The beggar lurked outside the *pandal*, hoping to scrounge some *prasad* from some kind visitor. He was shooed away every time he attempted to enter there so just outside seemed to be a more likely spot for him to get anything of the *prasad*. No one quite knew his name though he was a familiar figure around the station[78]. Dark, thin, with unkempt hair and bushy beard, both sprinkled with grey, eyes that spoke volumes, dirty nails and a tattered wrap completed his appearance. He had a cloth bag that was even more tattered, stuffed with God alone knew what. He looked hopefully at the various people exiting the *pandal*, packets of *prasad* in hand but none even looked at him leave alone offering him any. He waited, his hope undying for that was the only thing that he actually possessed. Sometime later, he noticed a young married woman of kindly appearance—he could tell this quality—coming out of the *pandal*, her husband behind, talking to some people. She caught his eyes and smiled as kindly at him, nodding, and gesturing with a packet in her hand. The signal was clear. He hurried up and cupped his palms to receive the packet from her. She dropped it in his hands, smiled sweetly again and turned around to join her husband. The beggar

---

[78] Character appeared first in story no. 5, *Murda Jaga!*

wasted no time. He had to find a safe spot where he could eat the food undisturbed. He swung towards the platform ahead of him.

The rush around the 8 Patna-Gaya passenger had abated greatly. Phani still stood at the handrail, smoking a cigarette, regret coursing strongly through him for he yearned a quick *darshan*[79] at the *puja pandal*. But there was no reliever in sight to who he could handover for a few minutes. His train was scheduled for the return trip to Gaya at 2300 hours and he would be finally done with his responsibilities. By then it would be quite late of course… He sighed again to himself. If only…

"*Arre* Phani-*babu*!" He heard someone hailing him.

"Sukhiya! What's going on with you? On leave?"

Sukhiya came up closer and stood on the platform opposite Phani. "Yes, sir, I'm off duty now…" He grinned. "Why aren't you going to the *pandal*?"

"I'm the driver on duty, Sukhiya… I can't go now!" He sighed again. "After that, surely…"

The liquor-induced benevolence was still sloshing inside Sukhiya. He hurried to offer Phani a quick solution.

"*Arre*! Why worry when I am here? I'll stay in the driver's cabin of your train and mind it so that you can make a quick visit to the *pandal*! That's the simplest solution!"

It was so tempting that Phani was forced to consider the offer. Dare he? It would really take no more than ten minutes for him to run across to the *pandal*. Surely Sukhiya could spell him for those few minutes? His train, rebadged as the 9 Patna-Gaya passenger, would start once the engine was removed and reattached at the other end, much after the Rajdhani departed. As for his offer, he knew Sukhiya,

---

[79] Literally, glimpse; in this scenario, paying obeisance to the presiding deity in the puja pandal or temple

a regular shuntman at this station, piloting engines to and from the loco shed. Phani made up his mind. He would take up Sukhiya's kind offer and be back before anyone knew! He got down from his engine, face wreathed in a grateful smile.

"Thank you, Sukhiya! I'll run over and be back in just a few minutes! Hold my train, please..." With a pat on Sukhiya's back and scant attention to anything else, he hurried off towards the *pandal* beckoning him.

Sukhiya cleverly stepped back as Phani rushed past him to avoid letting the latter smell alcohol on him, though he had chewed on several cardamoms and cloves. He waved Phani off and then slowly climbed aboard the engine. He looked around the cabin and rubbed his hands in glee. Finally, he was doing some good for his fellowman!

Meanwhile, Sukamal had the required green signal for him to berth at the allotted spot on platform 4, only a few minutes behind the scheduled arrival time of 2145 hours. He stepped out on the platform—permitted by rules—to await collecting the caution order from the ASM's office. This mandatory document provided the speed restrictions to be adhered to until the next stop station, Mughalsarai, where he would get the next caution order. He stretched, twisting this way and that, raising his arms straight out and arching his back... he heard a few joints crack; they were so relaxing! He smiled and looked around himself. A few passengers alighted at Patna on the way up to Delhi though there would be many more boarding. He watched those scurrying to their coaches and tapped his foot impatiently, waiting for the porter to come from the ASM's office with the caution order.

Meanwhile, the do-gooder spirit was wearing thin rather rapidly for Sukhiya as he paced inside the cramped driving cabin of the 8 PG. He wished he had remembered to also fill his hip flask—a plain glass bottle, to be sure. He could have used a good swig or two. He slammed the counter in a sharp mood swing and promised himself another round of drink back at the local liquor shack the moment Phani returned. Why was he taking so long anyway? He drummed his fingers, cursing his sudden dry throat. He spied Phani's bottle of water in one corner and while turning towards that, slipped on a spot of oil. He stumbled, and threw his hand out to grab something but couldn't find anything. His hand struck the GF[80] switch on the panel and it turned on, priming the main drive unit of the engine. Sukhiya prevented himself from falling after he slammed on the counter, but his hand then hit the starting gear, pushing it to the 4th notch. The starting gear controlled the speed of the engine's forward movement and the 4th notch meant the maximum speed of 110 kmph. The engine was now a missile. And it took off just like one.

Later, nobody could quite remember what they had been doing when it happened. Everything since the event was a blur; someone remembered something that was quite differently remembered by someone else. It was surreal. Strangely, it was the drunken perpetrator who had clarity of thought and even action.

The 8 PG passenger took off like a scalded cat. One moment it was standing still, the next, it was off. The distance between the engine and that of the Rajdhani's was barely 15 metres—some 49-odd feet—but the acceleration was stupendous, and it must have gained close to 35-40 kmph velocity when it hit the engine of the Rajdhani head-on. The resulting noise of the crash resounded all over. Then with a rending, wrenching metallic shriek, it climbed up over the Rajdhani's engine, the tremendous momentum causing it to rise at an angle of almost 45 degrees and slamming into the foot overbridge that was just behind, breaking chunks of concrete off it, and then stopped there, shuddering, precariously poised on top of the Rajdhani engine.

---

[80] Generator Field: Switches the field of the Exiter generator thus indirectly switching the main generator field

The impact of the crash caused grievous damage to the coaches of both the trains. Couple of design aspects saved the Rajdhani from worse than likely damage. One, the sequence of coaches: Passenger coaches were placed after the brake van and pantry car, and two, the crumple zones at either end of each passenger coach helped absorb the brunt of the impact. Only a couple of these coaches derailed. The 8PG fared worse: The brake van situated immediately behind the engine, was severely compacted, extensively damaged. Since the engine had climbed at an angle, the brake van too had tilted and hung twisted and mangled. Behind the brake van, four or five of the passenger compartments derailed but thankfully, none was occupied.

Sukhiya demonstrated amazing clarity of thought and action towards self-preservation though markedly less towards preventing or even minimizing the impact of the crash. The moment the engine roared to full life, he turned and jumped nimbly off the driver's cabin onto the platform and ran off without a backward glance as the train hurtled towards the stationary Rajdhani, disappearing like a wraith.

People on the platform had scattered like splattering raindrops. People on other platforms just stood there gaping after the initial ducking and falling flat on the ground when the tremendous reverberations rang through the entire station and surroundings. It took several minutes for everyone around to wrap their minds around the catastrophic event. The Senior Station Manager on duty that evening, Shyam Sundar, was on platform 1, along with the Union Railway Minster visiting there. There were several senior railway officials, divisional managers and operation managers, who were unsurprisingly accompanying the minister. The ASM, Ravindra Sekhar, had just issued the caution order for the Rajdhani and was hurrying up to the high-profile group to join them. Such visits were fraught with tension for obvious reasons though things had been going well till then. When the loud crash resounded, the minister's bodyguards hurriedly covered him up, looking for the safest place for their charge.

Meanwhile, the hubbub slowly started building, cries rend the air, the site turning into a chaos of confusion and shock. Shyam Sundar, who had crouched down initially, sprang up and looked about in some indecision, eyes wide with shock.

This was an emergency of the first order, needing immediate, urgent attention and action. Someone with a cool head needed to direct the operations necessary to untangle the gigantic mess, assess damage but above all else, save people who might be trapped in those coaches impacted, dead or worse, dying, maimed, for whom time to treatment was vital to survive.

The minister had recovered quickly, and grabbing the arm of the person nearest to him, Shyam, he cried, "Quick! Organize relief work!"

Shyam Sundar nodded and clutched hold of Ravindra, who had also sprawled close to him. "Let's go!" he yelled above the tumult. They ran towards their office.

The next few minutes still crawled, with confusion and chaos paramount, though a buzz seemed to be growing, indistinct but discernibly angry in tone. The senior divisional manager caught hold of a dazed porter and instructed him to get the station manager. The porter staggered off but was back within the minute.

"*Sahib*! SM-*sahib* isn't there! Nor is the ASM-*sahib*!" The porter was visibly shaken.

A brief search established that neither the SM and nor the ASM were anywhere in the station; they were paged but to no avail.

The senior Divisional Operations Manager immediately instructed the porter to fetch Manab Banerjee, the Sr. SM who was supposed to relieve Shyam Sundar from 2200 hours, now only minutes away. The porter hurried away.

Manab had by then dropped Mita off at home and was gobbling a very hurried dinner when the loud crash interrupted him. He dropped everything and rushed to leave for the station. His duty hours were about to start from 2200 hours anyway. As he was exiting, he found Ramsaran panting at his doorstep, pointing wordlessly back at the station with a finger that was visibly shaking.

They started running in silence.

The next few hours were a blur of concentrated effort at relief and rescue, with strong accent on the latter. Upon reaching the station Manab met the senior officials and the minister. The divisional operations manager gave him a free hand to deal with the catastrophe. There were of course the standard railway rules and procedures to follow but Manab could commandeer and deploy resources the way he deemed best. One of the priority objectives was to ascertain any loss of life. And considering the horrendous appearance of the crash, it was natural to expect several deaths. The rescue workers paid the most attention to listening for noises made by people trapped somewhere in those mangled ruins of the coaches, thumps, drumming sounds or even hails… but they heard nothing. The workers hacked through the crumpled metal of the coaches, shouted for anyone trapped but all such effort continued to elude success.

The Rajdhani coaches had passengers inside and there were injuries of course. Emergency aid had been organized, a couple of hospitals nearby had been alerted to receive those with injuries that needed further medical attention, and ambulances were requisitioned. There were a few people with joint dislocations, a fractured leg here and a broken arm there. There were a few head-injury cases too, but all-in-all, the extent of injuries was relatively low, especially when compared the horrific *appearance* of the disaster. The absence of death was unusual though most welcome. Any death would automatically constitute a Railway Board case with extensive enquiries and more stringent consequences and even reprisals.

Sukamal Dastidar had been thrown a few feet on the platform he knew not how. Barring a severe bruise on one arm and a couple of cuts here and there, he was physically unharmed; he was after all on the platform, several feet away from the engine and the impact. He was concussed and in shock but that was only expected. He had even started assisting in the relief and rescue work in some small measure. Phani had returned directly upon hearing the tremendous crash and had immediately gone into shock seeing his train in a pile-up that looked like a montage from hell. The realization had struck him right away of his culpability for this accident. It was *his* train, he *was* the driver on duty and it had happened on *his* watch. It was perhaps only human for him to think he had handed over, however temporarily and unofficially, to the shuntman Sukhiya; what had he done to end up in this situation in a matter of minutes?

Phani was of course questioned urgently by the senior officials, with—understandable—significant prejudice, of his "deserting" his train, leaving it unattended. Phani explained in disjointed sentences that he hadn't quite left it unattended but had Sukhiya to look after it until he came back in a few minutes. Manab, who was running here, there, and everywhere, was instructed to roust out Sukhiya. Ramsaran was pressed into service and he went off looking for him. Meanwhile, the GRP was brought into the case, as was the rule. A case would be made against Phani as *prima facie*, he was the driver on duty of the train that caused the accident and his negligence was manifest.

As in every case of accident, besides human relief and rescue, the other chief objective was to restore traffic at the earliest. The first thing was of course to divert all possible traffic on to non-affected tracks, and using the other platforms. The lines that were blocked to traffic were 6 and 8. The Home, Starter and Advanced Starter signal houses were instructed about these diversions so that they could advise trains accordingly. Manab then focussed on clearing lines 6 and 8.

He had requisitioned an Accident Relief Train (ART) from Danapur, the divisional headquarters, which formed the backbone of the operation and especially the retrieval of the capsized engine of the

8 PG. Powerful cranes had been deployed to extricate that engine off the Rajdhani. Other cranes were at work to pick up the derailed coaches, particularly of the 8PG as that had by then proved to be entirely unoccupied, reconfirmed with its planned departure time of 2300 hours, which was more than an hour away from the time of the accident.

The mood of the rescue team was a little upbeat since there had been no deaths. A major crisis seemed to have been averted. They worked with a will, ensuring all injured passengers were given succour, medical aid, and hospitalization where needed. The station had been cleared of all gawkers and non-passengers and the GRP had set up barricades to prevent unauthorised and unnecessary entries. The Rajdhani passengers and the incoming ones for the 9PG had been moved to the waiting halls and food and tea had been provided. All passengers, including the ones not of these two trains, had been informed of the delay in full resumption of services. The minister had also left after being satisfied that all was being done that needed to be done. He had promised further support.

Meanwhile, Sukhiya was found and hauled up before the railway officials. He had been drinking and seemed unable to stand upright without support. Phani was also present during this and fairly lit into Sukhiya demanding to know what mischief had he committed to have caused this mishap. Phani was restrained from getting violent by the others and warned to keep quiet. The divisional operations manager, Sikander Alam, then took up the questioning.

"So, Sukhiya, what did you do inside the cabin?" Sikander asked, deliberately posing the question that implied he knew and believed that Sukhiya had relieved Phani even if unofficially and for a short duration.

Unsteady and bleary-eyed but otherwise alert, Sukhiya denied outright that he had been anywhere near 8PG. There was stunned silence.

"No sir, I was never here... I am off-duty today, why would I do something like this, *sahib*?"

Despite the restraints Phani went almost apoplectic at this downright lie. However, Sukhiya remained steadfast in his denials, his drunkenness notwithstanding. Nothing worked to make him admit. They tried to find someone, anyone who had seen Sukhiya on the platform before the accident, but he seemed to have the devil's own luck: no one had seen him. The GRP inspector, Shalin Singh, threatened him with dire consequences but still to no avail. Sukhiya could not be budged. They had to reluctantly let Sukhiya go but Shalin warned him to be available at a moment's notice.

Manab was still constantly on the move, supervising, authorizing, guiding, and helping, completely focussed on the earliest restoration of services at the station. He was untiring, relentless, and seemed to be everywhere at once, even popping in for a few minutes during Sukhiya's interrogation. When other aspects appeared to have been brought mostly under control he directed his energies fully at extricating the 8PG engine.

The biggest, most powerful crane was being positioned for the purpose. While the ART team was the expert, Manab couldn't keep away from this crucial step in restoring services. Powerful arc lamps were strung to light up the precise spot. Manab was walking around with the ART members below the grotesquely, almost obscenely unnaturally positioned 8PG engine. The brake van looked as if it had been squashed by a massive hammer from the front, which indeed it was when the engine abruptly halted atop the Rajdhani and it slammed into the rear of the engine with tremendous force. The metal sheets resembled a bedsheet with haphazard folds, as if it had been carelessly thrown over the back of a chair.

The consensus was that the brake van had to be decoupled and lowered while the big crane would hold the 8PG engine in its powerful grip. Once some space was made, the engine would be gently lowered. The ART members were deciding the grip-points on the brake van, passing back and forth from under it since it too was raised a few feet above the rails. Manab too passed under and then once things were finalized, he decided to get back up on the platform from the tracks. He bent low and stepped under, intent on springing up onto the platform, when suddenly he felt drops of something on his bare left arm. He paid scant attention, caught hold of the edge of the platform and clambered up. As he stood there, unconsciously wiping that drop off his arm, Ramsaran, also standing close by, exclaimed loudly,

"Blood! *Sahib*!"

"Eh?" Manab looked at Ramsaran then followed his pointing finger back on to his arm. A bloody smudge ran from the top of his forearm to almost his wrist. He looked at his palm. It too was smeared in red.

His first reaction was, had he hurt himself? Was that his own blood? He quickly felt himself. No, there was no pain anywhere, no injury. The realization was electric.

"Stop!" He screamed at the top of his voice. "Stop!" He ran toward the ART members, gesturing wildly at them. "Stop!" he shouted again.

All people ceased work and stood gaping at him.

His voice raised still, he yelled, "There's somebody in that brake van!" He jabbed his forefinger repeatedly at the direction of the brake van. "There's blood dripping off it!"

For there could be no other explanation. For some reason, they had discounted the brake van in their searches as it was reported to be empty by Phani, the guard was supposed to have stepped off. Had he then not...?

The nature of the operation changed. Now they had to look for a person, and they had to do that with care. The probability of grievous injury was far higher, and death a distinct possibility. What would they find?

Workers with metal cutters, axes and crowbars now examined the mangled remains to determine the best access possible. Soon, they were at it, cutting, hacking, and making their way inside. They made a suitable breach in some time, and shone their lamps inside.

It was awash with blood. It had pooled, mostly congealed, and only a thick strand had found a convoluted path to flow sluggishly and drip from one corner of the doorframe. But of the body there was no sign. Yet. They had to cut through more. But it was evident where they had to cut through to: the core of the impacted end, the front end.

It didn't take long to reach there. But there was hardly anything to rescue. All that could be made out was that it had been a human. There could be no further identification possible for there was nothing left to work on for that purpose. The mangling was comprehensive, grisly, and lumpy. Several workers, including Manab and Ramsaran, retched, then cleaned themselves up. A couple of volunteers, with hardier constitutions, went to remove the remains. They also discovered a blood-soaked bundle that contained a few pitiful rags, an aluminium mug now squashed unrecognizably, and a few other knick-knacks.

It was Ramsaran who offered a possible identification of the pathetic remains based on the contents of the bundle: The unnamed beggar who frequented the station and was regularly chased away from everywhere he went. Gradually the possible course of events leading up to this terrible mishap was tentatively agreed upon: The beggar must have decided to slip into the brake van once he saw the guard leaving to either sleep or eat, undisturbed, or perhaps both. To a gruesome end.

This miserable discovery naturally changed the situation. A death had occurred, and it would mean a Railway Board case after all. Granted it was the death of a beggar, neither a railway staff, nor other workers and certainly not a passenger. But the rules were to be followed without concession. The outcome of the enquiry would be critical and the penalty, severe.

After this, Manab oversaw the removal of the damaged coaches and the engines. The damaged compartments were then hauled to the loco shed, and fresh ones were pressed into service. It was many hours before these could be arranged and the trains could depart.

By the time Manab could go home for a few hours of desperately needed sleep, he was reduced to a zombie-like state, running on empty and a string of cups of tea. He was back at work after a few hours for there was plenty to be done to complete formalities. It was further established that the then SM and the ASM had indeed run away and had not been traced since then.

The Railway Board enquiry dragged on for close on to year and a half. Shyam Sundar and Ravindra Sekhar were apprehended in their home towns within a few days of the incident. They had apparently run away with all their papers that night immediately after being asked to organize the relief and rescue work as they feared an angry crowd and a possible beating. Shyam Sundar lost his job while Ravindra Sekhar was dealt with a little more leniently: he was deprived of his annual increment for three years. Phani was found guilty but that amiable man, just 2 years away from retirement with full benefits, died in shock before the final decision of the Board was made. However, nothing could be proved against Sukhiya, the main perpetrator of the horrific accident and he carried on working there as a shuntman though he certainly lost a lot of goodwill, friends, and respect.

There was sympathy among the station staff and other workers for Shyam Sundar. Manab too felt it was understandable why he ran away; panic can cause irrational decisions. Railway staff getting beaten up for less was not unknown. Manab organized an informal donation drive for Shyam Sundar so that he could meet his family expenses. So, every pay day, sympathizers would donate some money and the collection would be handed over to Shyam Sundar. This went on for three years. Shyam Sundar appealed his case and ten years after the accident he was re-employed with the Railways, but he had to forego his seniority, interim pay hikes and other benefits that normally accrued from continued service.

10

The Hoarding

It had been raining steadily since late afternoon, the skies grey and foreboding. The rain wasn't hard but appeared to not be anywhere near letting up. Early evening, a breeze sprang up that quickly graduated to a frisky wind, gusting occasionally to rattle a few metal sheets somewhere or the other. It certainly looked like it could worsen as night crept up.

As the wet day darkened to a wetter evening, the new Rajendra Nagar Terminal station in Patna glistened in the rain under the lights popping on all over. This station had been inaugurated on the last day of March in 2003, a little more than a couple of years earlier. The purpose was to decongest the overburdened Patna Junction station. Along with two other stations on this busy main line, this new station and the venerable Patna Junction served the needs of hundreds of thousands of passengers through the year. This new station was modern with all conveniences that were deemed necessary then; it was the pride of East Central Railway zone.

Manab had been handpicked by the then union railway minster to head this gleaming station. And so Manab served as the Station Manager there. It was eleven years since that terrible accident at the Patna Junction station when the Patna-Gaya passenger had collided with the Howrah-Delhi Rajdhani. Manab's career had continued to progress well, earning him commendations, awards, honourable mentions in confidential reports, and of course, promotions too. He had been made station manager in 2000 and given charge of Fatuha Junction, another small station on the Howrah-Delhi main line within the Patna metropolitan region. After three years, he was brought in as the manager for the newly launched Rajendra Nagar station but had been recalled to Patna Junction a year later. In 2005 he was finally brought back to Rajendra Nagar on the express wish of the union railway minister and this was where he would finally retire in 2011, the same station where he would be reunited with Biswas and the foundling boy Uday in 2006.

His ability to interact with people at their level, and often in their language, to sympathise and yet not yield to unreasonable demands, and the repeatedly demonstrated skill of getting the job done under trying circumstances had brought him into notice of many senior railway officials and even the union minster for railways. This quality, as it often happened in life, cut both ways, bringing him approbation and sometimes envy. He had no complaints; he took life as it came, cherishing the good times, and downplaying the not so good. On the personal front, too, his children—Keya had grown up quite a bit, and twin siblings, a boy, and a girl—and his wife, Mita, were doing well.

Manab was at his desk, his files open in front, a cup of tea neglected on one side, a smouldering cigarette between his fingers and a phone receiver gripped between his left ear and left shoulder, busy making notes on a piece of paper. He had a conference coming up in Calcutta in a week's time and there were a hundred things that needed his attention to completion well before then. The continuous rain that day had also caused some disruption to the smooth flow of traffic outside; passengers were reaching the station late to board their trains, resulting in some instances of chain-pulling, delaying departures. The biggest irritant was the dirt and filth that invaded the otherwise clean premises with the multitudes trooping inside. Cleaners were deployed continually to cope with this. However, his ASMs were managing these aspects leaving him freer to deal with items that needed tactical decisions.

He disconnected the phone, reviewed his notes, and picked up the phone again, this time to dial out a number that he knew by heart. As he heard the phone ring at the other end, he looked out of the window, seeing the dark sky, laced by lightning bolts that barely rumbled. The wind seemed to be picking up speed still as he heard it whistle outside.

Far above, on the roof of the third floor of the station, the large hoarding that advertised a prominent brand of furnishing, "Calcutta Colours[81]" swayed and creaked in the wind. The hoarding was placed such that it faced out over the entrance to maximise visibility for all incoming traffic into the station as well as those passing by. On the face of it, the hoarding was a sturdy structure, flex sheet mounted on an iron frame measuring twenty feet by twelve, with the iron feet of the frame shod in concrete shoes. However, rust had almost entirely eaten up the left arm, and as the wind rose in ferocity, it shuddered with the strain, metallic shrieks going unheard in the general din of the rain, wind, and the trains that made enough noise to drown out most other sounds. As evening crept by and night slipped in, the wind increased in violence, though the rain slackened marginally. The hoarding was starting to bend increasingly from its weakened side, its metallic shrieks still unnoticed.

By the time Manab could wind up for the day and think of leaving, the wind had toned down a bit though the rain hadn't let up. He waited a while longer, hoping for it to abate a bit, reluctant to drive home in the pelting rain. Gone were the days when he lived next door to the Patna Junction station and going from one to the other was literally a matter of minutes. And yet the leg of mutton he had bought that morning implied a rather satisfying dinner and his stomach rumbled in anticipation. Oh, chuck it, he mumbled to himself. A quick sprint to the parking—which was in the open—and he could be off. Also, Mita would be waiting to have dinner with him, a meal they made it a point to have together unless he was held up, though he always called ahead if that happened. He hadn't done that tonight… he'd go. Just then the head porter sidled up to him.

---

[81] Brand name changed

"*Sahib*, aren't you planning to go home?" he asked.

The head porter, called Dhauliya—he was frequently ribbed for that, harking back to the eponymous small-time character in the hit movie *Sholay*—was a portly man, wearing a constantly worried look, as if he had just eaten something that disagreed with him. His tormentors used the same tone and dialogue as in that famous movie where a moustachioed dacoit had asked that character, "*Kya laye ho, Dhauliya?*[82]", continuing with the comment that this Dhauliya had remained worried since then as he hadn't answered that dreaded bandit to his satisfaction.

"Mmm?" Manab turned to look at his interlocutor and then went back to examining the unrelenting rains.

"Yes, Dhauliya… planning to run for it to the car…"

Dhauliya produced a dry umbrella—a rarity at that time considering the rain—and said, "I have an umbrella, *sahib*… I could offer you this…"

That would indeed aid Manab in getting to his car in somewhat dry a state. But he knew Dhauliya well. He laughed gently.

"Where do you need a drop, Dhauliya?"

The fellow had the grace to look embarrassed. "*Sahib*, Ratan's *paan* shop…"

Paan and Dhauliya were seldom apart. And everyone knew he had a running argument with Madan, the *paan* vendor on the main platform, on who made the better *paan*, he or Ratan. Madan had his followers and Ratan, his. The fight, though good-natured, was never ending.

"Okay, Dhauliya, let's go…" And they went off, Dhauliya springing open the umbrella and holding it above their heads.

---

[82] Literally, "What have you brought, Dhauliya?"; in the context of the movie, the bandit, who was illegally collecting food grains as their 'tax', was checking with him for his 'contribution'

Things quietened around the station significantly after 2300 hours. Most of the shops were closed, porters were mostly gone, with only a few passengers remaining. The rain had lessened but the wind had picked up even more pace, howling and shrieking in the night like a demented banshee, blowing even sodden sheets of newspaper occasionally and sometimes pieces of tin and other odds and ends. Outside, in the parking and the general frontage, the powerful lamps lit the area and one could see rain whirling in the wind, and rattling and crackling sounds all over. There were no vehicles there excepting one autorickshaw parked near a wall that ran perpendicular to the main building of the station. This wall acted as a barricade against the wind to an extent and perhaps that is why the driver had chosen that spot. He had pulled closed the canvas side covers, secured them to the frame with the thongs, curled up inside and wrapped in a sheet, fallen fast asleep.

Meanwhile, the hoarding above was bending ever more from its weakened spot, twisting and shuddering in the tension that built up with the wind straining against the flex sheet. Soon a corner was flapping vigorously having come undone. Suddenly, one of the pair of lamps that lit up the display flickered violently and then with a flash of light, sizzled and went out. The lone lamp continued to shine forlornly, swaying in consonance with the hoarding.

By midnight, the station had gone completely quiet. The rain fell still but now it fell almost horizontally with the power of the wind; it was a fully qualified storm. The shrieks were continuous, angry and vengeful. The lone lamp shining on the hoarding had also blown, leaving it in complete darkness. As the wind blew harder, the frame of the hoarding started to give way, the strain just too much for the defective arm to hold any longer. The flex had come apart further but the consequent ease in pressure was more than overcome by the increased wind speed. It was swaying crazily, dangerously. Finally, the left arm snapped with a wrenching sound and the hoarding careened over the edge of the roof, the enormous weight of the frame now on only one concrete base. The wind, as if with devilish intent, increased even more and the strain was just more than what the concrete base could hold; it cracked and blew apart as if a bomb had been lit inside. And the frame toppled from the roof, large, inimical, fatal, turning over and over, until it slammed into the parked autorickshaw, crushing the front half completely, and mangling the rear terribly. It crashed at last to the ground, evil done; the autorickshaw lay smashed, twisted, the front end flattened and obscenely raised towards the sky that continued to pour ruthlessly.

The harsh ringing of the telephone woke Mita up first, flustering her with its insistence while it was still dark. She rolled over to shake Manab awake. Being a light sleeper, he awoke quickly and trained by the years of his experience, came alert instantly. He walked quickly down to the hall to take the call. At this time of the night—a quick glance at the wall clock told him it was just after 0100 hours—it could only be work. And not good news.

"Hello?" he spoke into the receiver.

"SM-*sahib*! This is Mukesh! Mukesh Panwar!" The strident voice on the phone belonged to the night duty porter.

"Yes, I recognized your voice, Mukesh! Tell me, what's happened?"

The agitated man spoke in a rush. "*Sahib*! That *parde-wala*[83] hoarding has fallen down from the third-floor roof… and it has crushed an auto, and the driver—I think that's Biresh—is badly injured, bleeding heavily… and the hospital people are refusing to admit him!"

This came out quite disjointed and Manab had to ask Mukesh to slow down and repeat the entire thing, slowly. Finally, the message got through.

Manab immediately grasped the situation and its full possible import. Any death in such circumstances was filled with risk to railway property and personnel as crowds would gather and words

---

[83] Literally, "of curtains"; here, referencing the furnishings company's—Calcutta Colours—hoarding

would be tossed in anger and remonstration, and could quickly escalate to violence and rioting. It had potential to get very volatile.

"Mukesh, don't leave the hospital with Biresh under any circumstance! Hold there. I'll be there shortly!"

As he was driving back to the station a few short minutes later, he noticed the rain had almost ceased and the wind too had dropped to a gentle breeze. He drove through the dark streets with occasional streetlights, squelching over puddles and piles of garbage that had been displaced by the flowing rainwater.

The hospital that Mukesh had mentioned was really a private nursing home, named Modern Nursing Home, and only a couple of hundred metres away from the station; this was the closest medical facility. It was natural that the people would have taken Biresh there. When Manab reached there, he found the lobby crowded with more than a dozen locals with a handful surrounding a doctor, angrily demanding they admit Biresh. Manab spotted Biresh lying still on a gurney[84] in a corner, covered with a bedsheet that was entirely soaked with blood. Manab focussed on the doctor, whom he knew, Dr.. Sinha. Manab had helped him several times in the past with train tickets. He pushed through the crowd until he reached the doctor.

"Dr.. Sinha! Good to find you here!"

The doctor looked at him, startled a bit. Manab nodded at him and turned to face the crowd. He recognized a few faces—each a local, neighbours, so to say—while there was a bunch he didn't. He gestured at them all, palms raised.

"Listen, friends, please give me some space and some time. Let me speak to the doctor, please move to one side and wait patiently!"

The group stood quietly for a bit and then the people he knew murmured amongst them. Manab heard a few snatches, saying the

---

[84] Wheeled stretcher

station master-*sahib* would take care of things, now that he was there. The people edged to a corner. As Manab turned back towards the doctor, someone called out from the back.

"This is the fault of the railway! They'll have to set things right!"

Manab decided to ignore that for the moment since getting Biresh started on the treatment was more important.

Now the doctor, who had availed Manab's help many times in the past, was in a quandary. How could he deny Manab?

The doctor drew Manab further inside. Clearing his throat, he stammered.

"Mr. Banerjee, there are rules I cannot change!" The note of imploring in his voice told Manab it could be done.

"Doctor, you can see it's a matter of life and death… this crowd here will only grow and I cannot keep them from getting violent which could not only damage my station but also this hospital! Surely that risk is greater than some petty rules?"

The doctor understood the scenario, but he hesitated still. Manab anticipated his next point of resistance and moved to pre-empt that.

"Don't worry about the money, Dr. Sinha. I will provide my personal guarantee for that… you please start the treatment now! And I will also take care of the GRP."

Left with no credible reason to resist any longer, Dr. Sinha asked his staff to admit Biresh and they rushed him swiftly inside.

Having taken care of this urgent issue for the moment, Manab had next to get to the bottom of the mystery of the hoarding toppling over so tragically.

He found Rakesh Tiwari, the ASM on duty that night, fretting and worrying in the station. He had along with him a few others of the staff on duty for the night, prominent among them being Dhauliya, appearing more lugubrious than ever.

Relief flashed across the face of Rakesh for Manab was not only his superior officer but also had demonstrated abilities in tackling complex, even confounding situations. He poured out whatever little they had learned of the matter till then.

It was indeed little. Essentially, the storm had caused the hoarding to be uprooted and blown out over the roof and it had apparently fallen straight on the autorickshaw parked below, causing the mayhem it had done.

"There is no impact on the tracks, right? No obstructions to normal rail operations?" Manab's foremost concern was the movement of trains.

Rakesh confirmed there was none. Nothing of significance had happened on the inside of the station.

"Okay, then the next thing we have to do is to check the roof and the hoarding frame situation. Dhauliya, get a few torchlights and come with me. You too, Rakesh."

The roof had puddles of water which they did their best to avoid in the dancing beams of their torchlights. Reaching the spot, Manab ran his beam over the tortured, twisted iron frame, noting the left arm poking a rust-rotted metal finger at the sky, the edges torn as if with great force. To deduce it had been literally torn apart due to the storm was easy. He looked to the right side and immediately noticed the shattered concrete base. He bent low and examined it closely. It was wet, but it was discernible that it had burst into pieces as if pulled apart by some enormous weight. Was it even constructed properly? He poked around there for a bit to check if there was a provision to bolt the foot of the frame before pouring concrete over it. And found there was no such provision made. Just then his eyes were drawn to another spot about a foot from there. There was a metal baseplate bolted to the floor with a deep slot clearly available to slip a metal foot into and then bolted there. It was evidently another provision being readied to hold another hoarding. Quite clearly, concrete would be poured over that contraption to make it a far more solid base to hold a large hoarding. He looked to the left, seeking a similar base there too but didn't see one. However, he then noticed that the base of the broken arm of the frame had a differently shaped, more 'complete' looking concrete base.

While Dhauliya and Rakesh looked on without understanding, Manab stroked his chin as he thought this through. Why would the outdoor advertising company that had won the tender to erect hoardings in certain areas of the station, make provision for another frame to be installed but only on one side? Clearly it couldn't be for another hoarding at the same spot. For one, the new one would cover the existing one entirely, and for another, even if there was a plan to erect a second one at a different angle which wouldn't obstruct the existing one, it would not only detract eyeballs but also be incorrectly angled for maximum visibility from the roads. What was going on? He filed this away in his mind for the future; something told him it could be crucial information.

"Let's go," he said, getting up from his crouch. "Do you have anything to say?"

Neither had anything to add to what was evident: The concrete base had burst open causing the hoarding to topple over.

"They had done a shoddy job here, that's for sure," Rakesh asserted as they made their way back.

"I agree," Manab replied tersely for he fancied he heard some raised voices below. They quickly made their way down.

Downstairs, at the portico of the station, the crowd had reassembled though not yet as a coherent group, with any specific purpose. As Manab and the others reached there, Mukesh brought a man up to him.

"*Sahib*, this is Mungeri Lal… Biresh's *mama*…"

The man had a scraggly appearance, tousled hair, and jowls heavy with several days' worth of grey stubble, eyes lined with sleep, and now worry. He put his palms together in a *namaste*.

"*Namaste, sahib*! Biresh will survive, won't he?"

Manab laid a hand on his shoulder. "The doctors are working hard on Biresh now, *mama-ji*… don't worry for now. Let them work. Trust in God!"

The uncle nodded, sorrow etched on his face. "He's the only earning member of their family…" he murmured.

Mukesh then informed Manab that Biresh's father had passed away a few years ago, and Biresh with his autorickshaw was their only source of livelihood.

Just then a thin, dark man with a hooked nose, keen eyes and malnourished moustache came up. In a nasal voice that reeked of animosity, he opened his assault.

"Station Master! This will not do at all…"

Manab didn't like the vibes that man gave off right from the start.

The man held Mungeri Lal around his shoulders and picked up the thread.

"Look at this poor man! You've robbed him of his only son!"

That shot in the dark was clearly an exploratory attempt to fish in troubled waters. Manab controlled his temper.

He turned towards Mukesh. "Who is this man? He doesn't even know Biresh is not this man's son."

The thin fellow bristled at this deliberate slight.

"*Arre*! Why don't you ask me directly?"

Manab looked at the man. "Okay. Who are you?"

The man turned away from Manab, raised his arms and gestured at the people milling around there, hailing them loudly.

"Listen, all of you! Let's tell them very clearly that Railways cannot escape responsibility for this matter at all. And they'll have to give compensation to Biresh and his family!"

The men stopped their private chats and looked uncertainly at this man, a couple of them nodding. A few started moving up closer. Manab realised he had to pre-empt the situation building.

"Listen!" He raised his voice, and being taller than the thin trouble-maker, he had better visibility.

"Listen. Biresh is now admitted to the Modern Nursing Home. I personally have requested the doctor to take special care of him. Let us maintain peace and pray for his recovery." He noticed the thin man fidgeting to get attention back on himself so Manab continued in a firm voice.

"And I request all of you to go home now. Its two in the morning. Keeping awake will not help Biresh in any way. His *mama* is here. I've explained the situation to him and he understands it. I'll provide an update later after I speak to the doctor once the operation is over." He maintained eye contact with each member that was looking at him and held his voice at a soothing pitch but firm tone.

He nodded to them and turned to the uncle who had been standing behind, completely ignoring the thin man who was looking flustered at having his thunder stolen by a bit, and briefly gestured at Rakesh to ensure the people were gently but surely eased out of the station. Once outside, he hoped they would disperse peacefully. He then held Mungeri Lal by both his shoulders and spoke to him with sympathy.

"Mungeri Lal-ji, you also take some rest. I'll have Mukesh open a waiting room for you here. You rest there. I will keep you informed of how things progress… let's keep our hopes up! We shouldn't think negatively!"

He instructed Mukesh accordingly and as Mungeri Lal waited, a little overwhelmed by the attention given him, the thin man was seen gesticulating and trying to retain the people around him. Bolstered by Manab's head-on tackling of the situation, Rakesh too acted more confidently and with the help of a couple of other staff members, gently shepherded the people out. The thin man followed them out, clearly frustrated.

Manab was sure he hadn't seen the last of that trouble-maker; he'd be back. He now had other things to consider. The accident had happened in the station premises. The hoarding, while setup by a regular outdoor advertiser hired by a completely legal tendering process, was earning the station some rental revenue. If things took a turn for the worse, Railways would be implicated in some form. In any case, a case had to be registered with the GRP. Also, he wanted to speak to the advertiser regarding that frame. He swung to his office.

First things first, he needed to call the Assistant Divisional Railway Manager to inform him of the matter, despite the late hour. Lalatendu Jha was a man who always liked to be on top of situations and late news never sat well with him. He dialled his residence number.

Jha listened patiently to the entire incident then asked Manab to keep a close watch on Biresh's prognosis, and keep him updated on any need that arose. Next, he called the GRP officer in-charge Sunil Das and informed him of the case, asking him to register an FIR. By then Rakesh had returned to his office. After getting the latest update on the crowd situation—the people seemed to have dispersed for the moment though a few had remained, all outside—Manab instructed him of two things. One, to find out the antecedents of that thin man, and two, to call up the advertiser's contact person.

"What's his name again, this advertiser guy's?"

Rakesh scratched his head. "I think Ranjit... Ranjit something, sir," he replied apologetically.

"Okay, you confirm that and call that fellow, tell him that the shoddy work his company had done has resulted in grievous injury to one person... which could get worse..."

Rakesh looked at Manab with bulbous eyes. "Worse...? You think...?"

"No, I don't think so… not until I've spoken to the doctor again." Manab spoke firmly.

Rakesh nodded hesitantly. "But it's so late in the night… call him now? Or tomorrow morning?"

"Find out his mobile number and call him… now!" Manab wouldn't brook any delay if he'd help it.

Rakesh looked startled. Manab continued, remorseless.

"If that doesn't work, check if we have his residence number and call him on that. If that proves difficult, send a porter to his office tomorrow morning… it's not far, only Gandhi Maidan. Okay?"

Rakesh nodded but seemed reluctant to leave. Manab asked him, "What else?"

"Sir… My duty will end at 0600 hours. Should I ask Devesh to make that call?"

Devesh Tiwari was the ASM who would take over from Rakesh at that hour. Manab looked at him steadily, then spoke quite gently though the iron peeped through the velvet.

"Listen, Rakesh. This situation could very ugly very quickly and I'd certainly prefer you remain here a little longer to ensure Devesh comes to grips with the matter before you leave. Alright?"

"Yes, sir." Rakesh left, managing to maintain a stiff upper lip.

Manab looked at his watch. 0230 hours. An hour and a half since Biresh had been admitted. He thought of checking up on him. But he didn't take the main exit since the few people still there would likely follow him and he didn't want that. He slipped out from the parcel handling section and managed to sneak into the nursing home without being spotted. The lobby was empty excepting for a sleeping guard. He walked down the main corridor further inside hoping to find someone. The lone nurse dozing at the nurses' station knew him and upon being awakened, informed Manab that Dr. Sinha was yet to come out of the OT.

Manab considered. There was nothing for him at the station just yet; Rakesh could hold fort for now. Instead he decided to wait at the nursing home.

Almost thirty minutes had passed when the doctor came out and straightaway came over to Manab on seeing him waiting in a corner.

"Doesn't look good at all, Mr. Banerjee. He is in coma, there's been massive loss of blood, organs damaged, bones broken, but most critically, he has a grave head injury."

Dr. Sinha's synopsis was grim: Only a miracle could see Biresh survive.

It was not a question of supply of blood—always the favourite of movie makers—or of any specific organ. The overall damage was just too great. Another hour or two would tell.

"Please don't give any details of his condition to anyone, be they his relatives or anyone else."

This flustered the doctor. "How can I deny actual news to his relatives, should they come?"

Manab mission was to prevent any rioting and damage to the station and other railway property. He pleaded with the doctor.

"No, you don't have to lie to anyone, doctor. Just say that you are trying your best and will need some time to say anything for sure, that's all I ask. Meanwhile, I'll do what is needed to be done!"

The doctor nodded, a trifle unwillingly. "Should I come back in an hour or so to check status with you?" When Sinha nodded again, Manab concluded by saying, "Please call me if there is anything urgent, okay?"

Back at the station using the same route, again eluding everyone, he found Rakesh waiting for him.

"Sir, Ranjit Thakur… his mobile is switched off… maybe for the night. And there is no residence number either… we'll have to wait till the morning to get him."

Manab thought for a moment. "We do have his residence address?" When Rakesh nodded, he continued, "Send Dhauliya to his residence at 6 o'clock. Get that fellow here."

"Six in the morning, sir?" Rakesh's reluctance was apparent.

"Yes. That fellow has a lot to answer for," Manab replied, staring straight at Rakesh.

The next couple of hours passed slowly, or so it seemed to Manab. He had called up the doctor around 0345 hours and learned there was no change for the better. The doctor sounded even more despondent. He again called him up after 0500 hours and the doctor sounded even more frantic, barely giving him a minute to tell him that Biresh was sinking and they were trying their best to revive him.

Manab drummed his fingers on the table for a minute then dialled the ADRM, who picked the phone as if he was sitting next to it. Even his voice was keen.

"Yes, Manab?" He didn't even ask to confirm identity.

Manab briefed him on the deteriorating situation and that the doctor was holding out less and less hope of survival.

"Sir," said Manab. "Please sanction the fifteen thousand rupees *ex gratia* compensation from your accident relief fund. I am expecting some trouble once the announcement is made. If I am able to offer some compensation at that crucial moment…" he left it unsaid for it was obvious.

"Hmm… you've tried to get hold of the advertiser fellow?"

"Yes, sir. I'll have him in my office soon after 0600 hours."

"Hmm… okay. I'm sanctioning that fifteen thousand and will send that across with my peon shortly."

"Thank you, sir! That is really very helpful." Manab was relieved to have succeeded in getting the ADRM's approval.

"Keep me informed," Jha concluded and disconnected.

As if on cue, the thin man barged into his office along with a couple of other men, all looking aggressive. Rakesh and Dhauliya hurried in after them, hassled, and berating them. But before they could speak to Manab, the thin man opened up.

"Station Master!" The way he uttered it made it sound like a rebuke.

Manab raised his palm, face grim. "Quiet!" His voice cut like a whiplash. The thin man looked taken aback, mouth working silently.

"First, you tell me who are you and what business is this of yours?"

The thin man blustered. "I am *Chhotte Bhaiya*[85]! I am an important worker in the Lok Seva Party[86]!" Calling himself important was a dead giveaway of course.

Manab smiled despite himself. "That's hardly your name. What is your name? And what is this to you?" He asked these peaceably though he knew the real answer to his second question: Chhotte Bhaiya was out to make his name off this mishap.

Chhotte Bhaiya's expression was a sight. Disbelief couldn't be expressed more eloquently. "People know me well as that… though my name is Monu Sahay."

Manab leaned back in his chair. "And?" He drawled the follow-up question.

Chhote Bhaiya took another few seconds to recover. Then he reverted to his norm: He blustered, self-importance dripping.

"These are my people! They look up to me to provide them leadership, to guide them! And when one of my people is hurt, why, I'll speak up for him! Compensation is obvious, else…" He stopped and glared.

With a calmness that he wanted to shred, Manab replied, in slow and distinct tones.

____

[85] Literally, 'Younger Brother'; clearly, this was a nickname
[86] Name changed

"Mr. Sahay. One, don't bring politics into an accident. Two, nothing is obvious. Three, Biresh is in hospital, the doctors are trying their best to save him. Everyone here is aware of these so there is no need for leadership or direction right now."

Manab deliberately ignored that veiled intent of threat in Sahay's 'else'.

The thin junior politico struggled to keep control of the situation. "And compensation?"

Manab ignored the politician again. He asked Rakesh, "How many people are outside?"

"Er… quite a few, sir. Maybe twenty or thirty? I'm not sure…" Rakesh was silently admiring Manab's handling of this pesky politician.

Before Sahay could react, Manab sprang up from his seat and walked briskly out, the others in tow, Sahay straggling behind in some bewilderment.

There was a bunch of people again milling around the entrance lobby. Manab herded them out into the early light of breaking dawn and requested them with word and gesture to step down below the few stairs. Then he stood on top of the staircase and raised his voice.

"Thank you for waiting so patiently for news on Biresh's health. I've been in constant touch with the doctors at the nursing home. They are still working. The injuries were grievous and require extensive surgeries. This will take time. Meanwhile, you know Indian Railways is very concerned about these types of situations and always steps forward to provide support to victims and their families, in all manners possible." He paused for breath, looking toward all the assembled people, trying to read their expressions. They appeared calm, even considerate… and to his eyes, believing in him. He took the next step at keeping the politician out of the game to the extent possible.

"I've also spoken to my senior management regarding some possible compensation." He paused again, looking closely at the people. The magic word had been uttered in their presence, compensation. From the corner of his eye, he thought he saw Sahay's face registering anger at having been undermined, the possible good news being directly delivered to the people instead of through him when he could have made it appear as the outcome of his effort alone.

Manab continued. "Now you know that Railways is a huge organization, things take a little time. Every action has a process, approvals and permissions and sanctions… I have requested for this already and I hope to get the good news soon. However, the money itself will take a little while longer to come through… remember, the accident happened in the night… everything was closed then. Right?"

A chorus of 'yes' went up, a few smiles too. Someone, possibly Rakesh, had brought Mungeri Lal out as well, and Manab saw him smiling, some satisfaction in his expression. Whereas, Sahay's face was like a thundercloud.

Manab smiled briefly. "Please support me in this, I'll update you all when I have more news!" With that he stepped back, purposely not asking them to go home. It was dawn and people would find reasons to linger. As he went back inside, he noticed the people to be generally a little more relaxed and Sahay trying to speak to a few but being rebuffed.

The first thing he wanted to do next was to call the District Magistrate, Nakul Kumar, whom he knew well from several formal and a couple of informal occasions. As he was about to pick his desk phone it rang.

"Hello?" Dread ran through him.

"Mr. Banerjee?" It was Dr. Sinha. "Can you please come to the hospital?"

"Sure! What is it? Is Biresh…?"

Sinha cut him off. "Yes, but please come…" and disconnected.

Manab strode off, taking the parcel handling entrance. While he was hurrying there, he guessed there could be people in the hospital's lobby as well, so he took a side entrance, the ramp that was used for wheeled stretchers.

He found Dr. Sinha waiting near the OT who took him immediately by the arm and guided him to his chamber.

"Mr. Banerjee, I am sorry. We couldn't save Biresh. He died at 0540 hours." He made the announcement without any fanfare. His face was lined with exhaustion, eyes seemingly in hollows, and his voice barely above a whisper.

Though Manab was expecting this, the bald news nevertheless felt like a cold wash. He sat down in a chair. The first thing that struck him was the seeming inadequacy of the compensation he had managed to secure, fifteen thousand. The DM's contribution was going to be even more important now.

Then, he said, "What finally caused this, doctor?" He'd need this to explain to the waiting people.

"Too many organs were devastated… liver, one kidney, right lung pierced, veins and arteries severed… and that head injury… he had very little chance, anywhere. Only a miracle… perhaps…" The doctor's voice petered off.

While listening to him, Manab realised forcefully that he needed time before they could announce the death. He simply *had* to offer something along with that announcement.

"Dr. Sinha! I request you to not announce this news yet, not until I tell you to!" He was frantic.

The doctor looked stricken. "How can I not? That is crazy! The time is noted already! I cannot!"

Manab jumped up in his anxiety. "No, no! I am not requesting you to change the time of this death… just delay the announcement for some time, say anything… just buy me an hour or so… so that I can arrange for some vital stuff… I request you!"

The doctor needed some more persuasion before he agreed, very reluctantly. He agreed he would wait for Manab's call before declaring the news. Manab thanked him profusely, and promising to hurry things up as much as he could, he rushed back.

He caught hold of a worried looking Rakesh waiting for him in his office and instructed him to send Dhauliya to fetch the advertiser guy Ranjit right away.

"There's no point waiting to see if he's switched on his mobile… just send Dhauliya!"

Rakesh hurried off and he immediately called the District Magistrate, Nakul.Kumar.

The DM usually rose early, he knew, and went off to play tennis. He was sure he'd catch him before he left though he of course had his mobile number. The DM picked the phone himself and listened to Manab explain the incident in some detail, including Biresh's death.

"Sir, I'm confident I can prevent rioting and damage by offering something when we announce the death. The ADRM has already sanctioned the Rs15,000 relief amount. Your contribution…"

The DM had an *ex gratia* fund from which he could also give ten thousand rupees. This he mulled over for a few long seconds.

"I know you, Banerjee-*babu*, and I know how you work. Okay, I'm sanctioning this amount as well. I will deliver it personally on my way to the tennis club. Okay?"

Manab couldn't thank him enough. He cradled the receiver. Now he had twenty-five thousand rupees in the compensation kitty. Just then he heard loud wailing outside his office, and Rakesh came in, harried and tired.

"Sir, Biresh's mother and brother have come. They live in Panapur, across the Ganga, so it took time for them to reach here… they want to meet Biresh, sir…"

Rakesh of course didn't yet know of Biresh's death. He debated whether to keep him informed then decided against since that would be the best insurance against a premature leak.

He sighed heavily. "Okay, send them in…"

A frail, elderly woman wrapped in a plain white sari came in accompanied by a youth in his late teens, both looking dazed, the woman wailing continuously.

Manab and Rakesh spent the next few minutes settling them down, offering water, with Manab keeping up a soothing monologue. When they appeared a little relaxed, Manab spoke.

"I'm afraid it is difficult at this moment to visit Biresh. He is in the operation theatre… we cannot enter there, you understand me? Even I am not allowed inside. Wait a while longer, please."

Manab felt wrenched inside to imply Biresh was still alive but he needed some time… he was apprehensive of *Chhote Bhaiya*'s inclination for violence.

The woman had not ceased to weep though her wails had abated a bit. The young fellow, whose name was Biren, spoke hesitantly.

"*Sahib, bhaiya* will survive, won't he?"

Manab closed his eyes for a beat, despair clawing at them from inside.

"I really hope so. Let's pray he does…" He forcefully turned towards Rakesh. "Please take them to Mungeri Lal-ji in the waiting room, will you please, Rakesh?"

At this deliberate move, Rakesh took them away and returned soon.

"Sir? Is he alive?" His direct question was like an arrow. He couldn't dodge it.

"No. He died at 0540 hours."

Rakesh staggered. He caught hold of the table and sat down, something he never did unbidden in Manab's office.

Finally, he recovered enough to say, "And we're yet to announce this? There'll be violence!"

Manab's eyes blazed. He whacked the table sharply. "That is the reason we've not yet announced that. We need to offer something as compensation… I've got twenty-five thousand in the kitty and must find some more… Don't utter a word now! Not until I tell you to, okay?"

Rakesh gaped at Manab. That twenty-five thousand rupees had impressed him beyond words. He was aware the ADRM had a fifteen thousand limit; how had he arranged another ten, he wondered to himself.

Just then, as if to underline Rakesh's wonder, the DM himself walked in, followed by Dhauliya and another man who had evidently dressed very hastily, buttons miscued.

Manab jumped up and shook Nakul's extended hand. A fair-complexioned man of average height, Nakul played tennis to keep himself fit and it showed in his physique.

"Here's the ten, Banerjee-*babu*. I'll have the paperwork taken care of in the background. I'm very sorry to hear of that young man's death, my condolences…"

"Thank you so much sir, this really means a lot to us! Biresh's family is here and I'd have requested you to handover the money directly to them… but we are not ready yet. The ADRM's money is yet to reach here," Manab explained.

"That's alright, Banerjee-*babu*. You can take care of those things. Do you need me to arrange some additional policemen? For protection?"

"No, sir, the RPF has been deployed around the station perimeter… we should be okay for the moment. If there is any need I will definitely take your help, thank you again for the offer."

Nakul left soon after and Manab turned his attention to Ranjit, the man who had come along with Dhauliya, and waved at him to sit.

"You can go, Dhauliya," he said quietly and waited until that fellow left. Then he spoke to Ranjit.

"Have you heard about the matter yet, Ranjit, from Dhauliya?" The grim tone conveyed the seriousness of the issue in no uncertain terms.

"Y-yes," he stammered a little, nervously fingering his collar button.

"Well, that's compounded now. That young man is dead." He looked steadily at Ranjit, willing him to speak.

"Er… that's bad news, of course…" he paused but it was clear he was struggling to articulate something.

Manab waited. Silence could be very persuasive.

Ranjit gathered himself visibly. "Er… but I'm afraid I… mmm… don't understand how my company or I am… er… implicated!"

Manab continued looking at him steadily, eyes unblinking and the silence oppressive. It caused the tension to soar in the room; Ranjit inserted a finger inside his collar and moved it around in half-circles, his temples sweaty.

Finally, Manab broke the silence, his voice hardly above a whisper, almost sibilant.

"How are you implicated? I'll tell you. You installed that frame on the roof without making the right provisions. The right-side foot was just held by some concrete that burst when enormous, undue pressure was put on it."

As Ranjit made to protest this charge, his eyes wide, Manab continued. "And you didn't inspect the frame at all else you'd have known the left-side arm had rotted through with rust!"

Ranjit just gaped, silent.

"And," Manab now moved in for the sucker punch. "You *knew* the right-side foot needed a base clamp for it to be bolted into, but it hadn't been installed yet and you had your deadline to get that hoarding up… your client must have been hounding you… so you cut corners and made a temporary arrangement. Right?"

Ranjit said nothing, the silence more eloquent than any denial or explanation.

"Ranjit, I saw the other base clamp installed a foot away from the burst base… your plan was to move the hoarding slightly and fix the right-side foot there later… but you never found time to do that, did you? Had you done that…"

Ranjit stirred. He whispered, "The workmen broke the clamp they had brought that day while trying to bolt it to the floor of the roof… they had no spare clamps and the client was visiting the next day… I… I told them to get it up somehow…which they did… but… but…" his voice trailed off.

"And a man died for that negligence." Manab couldn't find sympathy for this man. He sighed.

"Two months and a bit, right, the hoarding's been up…? And you couldn't find time to fix that… targets, huh?"

Rakesh looked on in complete wonder. Ranjit shook himself.

"What do I do now…?"

Manab spoke in more normal tones. "See, this is a police case and they will have the full story. Your company will be charged… all these will happen. What you can do now is to try making up to some degree… maybe your generosity will make this a little easier…?"

"Generosity? What… what do you mean?"

"Announce a compensation amount of fifty thousand rupees… along with what I am gathering, it'll be a little meaningful."

"Fifty… thousand!" Ranjit sounded aghast. "I… I don't have that kind of authority!"

"Then call up your manager, speak to your seniors. Tell them what has happened, and the terrible press they will be getting. Think!"

"I'll be fired!" It came out almost as a moan.

"They'll listen to you since the company brand name will be pilloried. Speak to them!"

Ranjit squirmed, the weight of the revelation enormous on his shoulders. "I… I…"

Manab stood up. He pointed at the door. "Go. And speak to them!"

He motioned at Rakesh to take him out but Ranjit stood up and staggered out.

"Rakesh, go with him and stay there! Don't let him run away, restrain him by force if necessary!"

As he turned to go, Devesh came in, bewildered at the goings on, evidently still not in the full know of the case. Manab looked at him and said, "Devesh, good morning. Go with Rakesh. He'll tell you all. Keep quiet and listen to the full story and wait for me. Okay?"

Devesh nodded and then went out after Rakesh.

It struck him that the ADRM's peon was yet to arrive and he also had to update him of the latest developments. He called Jha. When he picked the phone, they spoke quietly for five minutes, Manab first briefing him on the complete developments since they had last spoken. At the end of the conversation, Manab reminded him of the peon's delay in arriving.

"Sir, your peon is yet to reach here… would you know by when he could arrive?"

"Oh, Manab, I forgot to mention this! He was on a bike and he had a puncture on the way. And this early he hasn't been able to find a shop to fix that. He assured me he'll reach you the soonest possible." Jha was apologetic.

"Oh, I see, sir! Never mind… sir, may I use the collection money to take the fifteen and I'll replace that amount when he arrives?"

Every station collects substantial cash in the form of different types of transactions, tickets purchase, penalties, fees, and so on and fifteen thousand wouldn't be a problem at all for an important station like Rajendra Nagar.

"Hmm… okay. Just write out a receipt and take that. When Govind, my peon, reaches, you replace that with the cash he is carrying. Okay." Jha's pragmatic approach to solving ground-level problems had made him popular with his juniors.

With that sorted out, he had to wait for a confirmation from Ranjit… at least he was hoping he would get a positive answer. Considering the display of gross negligence any opportunity towards compensating for that ought to be seized upon by them.

But could he wait any longer? He had twenty-five thousand ready, maybe approval for another fifty in a while. Could he wait?

He walked out to check on Ranjit and his juniors. He found Ranjit on his mobile talking and gesticulating, walking back and forth in great tension, while both Rakesh and Devesh stood by close, the former speaking steadily and the latter nodding.

It would take time for Ranjit to get his approval. Manab decided to wait no longer. He called Rakesh and Devesh over and told them his plan, then he walked back inside his office.

He called Dr. Sinha and told him to announce the death of Biresh. As he finished, Rakesh came in with the fifteen thousand in cash from the previous day's collection, which he had access to as the night shift ASM. Manab gave him a signed receipt for the same. Then he sat back and braced himself.

He didn't have to wait long. Dhauliya came in running, hair askew and panic writ large on his face.

"*Sahib*! The crowd is getting violent, they're threatening to break things!"

Manab was expecting this.

"Where's Inspector Naik?" The RPF inspector had taken charge of security of the station with the limited force at his disposal.

"Inspector-*sahib* is there, on the stairs while the crowd is getting restive around him, *sahib*!"

"And where's *chhote neta*[87]?"

Dhauliya looked alarmed. "He… he's there, *sahib*…"

He strode out with Rakesh and Dhauliya in tow. Pausing to instruct Devesh to keep a strict eye on Ranjit, who was still on the phone, he rushed to the portico staircase.

The crowd was perhaps no more than thirty, but they were very raucous, a few slogans rending the air, demanding compensation, and a few stray curses. Manab stood there and spotted the pesky politician, Sahay, who was working with great enthusiasm amongst the people. He also saw Biresh's family members there, surrounded by a few who appeared to be offering exaggerated sympathy.

Manab walked up to Naik first, and spoke quietly in his ear, telling him to post a few men near them, and then walked up to Sahay, touching him on his elbow. The man turned, surprise flashing on his face but quickly morphing into a leer, now that he had a death to play with.

"Master!" His seemed to have dispensed with even the prefix 'station' from his usual tirade opener.

"Now you'll see the power of *Chhote Bhaiya*!" he gloated.

Manab leaned close. "I have spoken to *Bade Bhaiya*[88]. I suggest you leave here. Else shut up and stay back. You get me?"

Chhote Bhaiya blanched at the implication of that other epithet. His eyes were struck with fear and he visibly shrank. While Manab was bluffing about having spoken to their main leader, it was true that he knew him, and more importantly, the leader was rather fond of Manab.

Manab closely observed this change. He pointed back over his shoulder, towards the entrance to the lobby, farthest from the crowd assembled at the portico. He went there slowly, licked.

[87] Here, 'small leader', contextually derogatory

[88] Elder brother; in this context, it implied the main leader of the party

Then Manab squared his shoulders and raised his voice, pushing back his exhaustion.

"Please listen! All of you, please listen!" He paused for some quiet. Then, when things seemed a mite quieter, he continued.

"All of you know that we couldn't save Biresh despite our best efforts. The doctors tried for several hours… but as you'd have heard from them, there were just too many organs damaged for him to be able pull through.

"I know this is tragic and words are… well, words. Sympathy feels nice for the moment but what of the future? We must think of the future! We have tried to provide some compensation right now… the details I'll share with Biresh's family, his mother, brother… his *mama*…"

A thought struck Manab just then. He called Rakesh and asked him to fetch Ranjit. When he went inside for that, Manab continued.

"Even the company that put up the hoarding, they understand the tragedy, they feel it too." He paused again, and watched the people. While they had been restive earlier, they were now a little quiet, digesting the news, dealing with the implied message that the Railways had their concern foremost in their mind and were trying to redress their grievance as best possible under the circumstances.

Rakesh came back with Ranjit and Devesh, still doggedly with his quarry. Ranjit had his mobile in hand, apparently called away mid-conversation. Manab pointed at Ranjit, and spoke again.

"You see this gentleman? That is the company man… he's trying his best as well to see what best he can do for Biresh's family! You see that?"

A few nods, a smile or two greeted this news. And this served to also put additional pressure on Ranjit, to try even harder.

Manab gestured at Devesh to take Ranjit back in; his purpose was served. He called Rakesh and told him to continue speaking to the crowd in the same vein while he would take Biresh's family inside and handover the money.

Biren and his mother were wreathed in tears, the latter also wracked by great sobs. Mungeri Lal appeared to be in better control. Manab addressed him.

"Mungeri Lal-ji, I will hand over the compensation amount to Biresh's mother, and I suggest you make arrangements for Biresh's funeral."

The *mama* looked blankly. Then a crafty look came on his face.

"How much money is that, *sahib*?"

"Twenty-five thousand." He said it very matter-of-factly.

Mungeri Lal's eyebrows rose. That was a large sum of money. Manab could read him like an open book.

"But I don't have money to arrange for the funeral… if you give that to me, I'll manage somehow…"

At this, the mother suddenly stopped her wailing, and in a high-pitched voice, she railed in *Magahi*.

"*Arre*, you want to take our money? What will we eat tomorrow we don't know! Can't you spend a few rupees for your nephew's funeral?"

The *mama* looked embarrassed but didn't offer money for that purpose. To prevent this from becoming a blocking issue, Manab offered:

"I'll give you some cash for the funeral purposes, okay? Separately… Please wait here." He went out along with Rakesh and in a few short minutes, collected enough money for a simple funeral. He put the cash in an envelope and handed it over to Mungeri Lal. He also put the twenty-five thousands in another envelope, sealed it and handed over to Biresh's mother after getting her thumb impression on a declaration of having received that money.

Then they left to claim the body and go for the cremation.

After they left, the crowd slowly dispersed. The exhaustion struck Manab, Rakesh, Dhauliya and everyone else who had been up through the night, and had dealt with the unbearable tension of a life and death matter, and the terrible consequence possible, even probable, with the wild card pesky politician to stir things up even more. Manab let Rakesh go home after cross-checking Devesh's grasp of the incident's details. By then Ranjit had also reached some decision on his predicament.

His manager and other senior people had grudgingly given in to the compensation demand of fifty thousand rupees. While Ranjit was in for difficult times ahead, his seniors had realised they had to do much to even hope for any redemption. Ranjit arranged for a formal note on his company's letterhead committing to donating Rupees Fifty Thousand towards the future security of Biresh's family in the form of a banker's cheque which would be handed over at a later date to either the mother or the brother.

Manab didn't feel like driving all the way home to freshen up; he was too tired for that. Instead, he freshened up at the station in the rather well-appointed toilet available for senior officials and used a fresh set of clothes—that he normally maintained in the office—to change into, feeling much cleaner. A few cups of tea and cigarettes gave him a semblance of normalcy.

He was also aware that Biresh's family would be back later in the day.

And they did come back, before sunset, the mother, brother, and the *mama*. Manab was prepared.

He had kept ready a photocopy of the commitment letter given by Ranjit. This he handed over to the mother after explaining the English wording in detail. The amount mentioned therein hushed their speech. But the *mama* thought farther.

"But *sahib*, money, however much it maybe now, will only last for a time… no regular income will mean that money will be spent and then they'll be left with nothing… then?"

Manab had anticipated exactly this.

"Yes, I know. That's why I propose to push for a job in Indian Railways for Biren. That'll be a permanent solution, wouldn't it?"

Manab wasn't sure at all if he could succeed but he would try for sure, even a class IV job, like Dhauliya or Mukesh. However, this proved to be extremely agreeable to everyone.

"So, who should I ask them to make the cheque to? Whose name?" Manab asked.

This brought up a sordid tussle between all three of them, the mother, Biren, Mungeri Lal. Each wanted the cheque in his or her name. The *mama* advised them that as their senior and being the most experienced among them, he could take the best care of the money. The mother scoffed at it and said he had never dealt with such a large sum in his life so how could he have that experience. The son alleged neither of them had a clue about banks, so they would be completely lost whereas he was young and knew all about banks—clearly an exaggeration—so he should have it. The mother poohpoohed it, saying she needed to have a support for the future at her age and in any case, Biren would get a Railway job so he would be set for life! It seemed to be going a little strident when Manab ended it with a decision: He would have it made in the mother's name, and arrange for a bank account if needed. This settled, they finally left. Manab could stretch his long legs and breathe a sigh of relief. The long day was finally at an end.

The cheque finally reached Biresh's mother three months later. Ranjit lost his job, the company was charged with negligence, and they lost their contract with Indian Railways. And sadly, Manab could not manage to get Biren a job as he was not educated enough nor interested to get educated to try for the job later; he just wanted it on a platter. That didn't happen.

The End